GOOD
GIRL,
BAD
GIRL

D0921252

WITHDRAWN
LEASIDE BRANCH

GOOD GIRL BAD GIRL

CHRISTOPHER FINCH

🐦THOMAS & MERCER

The characters and events portrayed in this book are fictitious. Any similarity to real persons, living or dead, is coincidental and not intended by the author.

Text copyright © 2013 Christopher Finch

All rights reserved.

Printed in the United States of America.

No part of this book may be reproduced, or stored in a retrieval system, or transmitted in any form or by any means, electronic, mechanical, photocopying, recording, or otherwise, without express written permission of the publisher.

Published by Thomas & Mercer
PO Box 400818
Las Vegas, NV 89140

ISBN-13: 9781611099713
ISBN-10: 1611099714
Library of Congress Control Number: 2012922331

For Linda

ONE

That was a tough year to be a New Yorker. The city was so broke there was a rumor going around that the mayor had been spotted on the Bowery, cleaning windshields at stoplights in the hope of scoring a nickel, or maybe a nickel bag. A garbage strike had turned the sidewalks of swank Upper East Side neighborhoods into urban compost heaps, heady with Camembert rinds and doggy bags chauffeured home from La Cote Basque. A turf war in the schools had black parents in dashikis and white teachers in high dudgeon slinging around words that don't show up in vocabulary tests. There were riots in Bed-Stuy, the South Bronx was a war zone, and a heroin epidemic was spreading like PCBs in the Hudson River. Central Park after sundown was a place you didn't go unless you had a thing for the taste of your own blood, but if you wanted to get mugged that could be arranged just about anywhere. It didn't help that the City's Finest were on a job slowdown, which meant that they spent less time responding to 911 calls, and more time padding their paunches at Famous Ray's Pizza. There were more than eleven hundred murders in New York that year. Even Andy Warhol got himself

1

gunned down. But, hungry for another fifteen minutes of fame, he hung on to defy the statistics.

I mention Andy because my office was on Union Square, a few doors from where Val plugged him. The Heartland Credit Union Building was an anonymous structure that attracted tenants seeking anonymity—unfrocked dentists, myopic eye doctors, low-life lawyers, assorted quacks, polyester-suited real estate shysters, vodka-soaked teachers of English as a second language, masseuses and manicurists with interesting sidelines. My hutch was on the third floor. If you cracked the solitary window open, you were overwhelmed by the aroma of sweet-and-sour pork deep-fried in peanut oil that should've been thrown out before Mao set out on the Long March.

It was one of the first uncomfortably hot days of the year—one of those May mornings when a tropical front breezes into town unannounced, like that cousin from Miami you hoped had lost your address. I was sitting at my desk, wallowing in this rank fragrance, indulging in my first toke of the morning, and trying to hear the daily napalm atrocity report on WBAI above the traffic and police sirens, when the phone rang. It was an attorney who identified himself as Joseph Bledstone of the firm Bledstone & Crimmins. He didn't beat around the bush.

"Mr. Novalis, I understand you were fired from your position as an investigator with the DA's office?"

No argument from me.

"Possession of marijuana. I presume you're clean now?"

"Whiter than the driven snow," I said, taking another hit.

Bledstone telegraphed his opinion of my attitude by pausing for a long beat.

"You were an investigator for the DA's fine art fraud detail?"

"I *was* the fine art fraud detail."

"Which means that you dealt with what kind of matters?"

"Fakes. Misrepresentation. Manipulation of auction prices. Is that the kind of malfeasance we're talking about?"

"Not precisely. I take it that you have a sound general knowledge of the inner workings of the art world."

"You mean, like how artists get screwed by dealers?"

"I mean, can I presume you are familiar with the art world's social mores?"

"You mean, who's fucking who?"

"Among other things."

This was beginning to sound interesting.

"Perhaps you'd better fill me in."

"Mr. Kravitz will brief you himself. Mr. Gabriel Kravitz. He'll be expecting you at his apartment in the Altamont Towers at six thirty."

Bledstone had nothing more to say, so we left it at that. I called Mike Pearson at the *Post* and asked if he knew anything about someone called Gabriel Kravitz. Mike said he'd check the morgue and get back to me. He called half an hour later, distracting me from the Yellow Pages where, in a desultory way, I was looking up companies that install room air conditioners, paying particular attention to ads that said, "Nobody Beats Our Rates."

"Steve on the business desk was able to help me out with your Mr. Kravitz. He served in the Pacific—made captain. When he was discharged, he came home to Cleveland, where his family owned a small construction business. He made his first fortune cashing in on the postwar building boom—those ticky-tack estates they built on swamps in the boonies—but he hit it big-time when Ike signed the Federal-Aid Highway Act into law. Kravitz got contracts to construct sections of interstates all over the Midwest. He's also the man behind Tomma-Hawk Motels. A couple of years ago, he made an unsuccessful bid to buy the Cleveland Indians, though why anyone would want to own those bums is beyond me. Mr. K's first wife—the proverbial high school sweetheart—divorced him, and presumably lived very comfortably ever after. About three minutes later, he married a former Miss Cuyahoga County, wherever or whatever that is. That was in 1949. These days, Mrs. K pops up on the gossip pages from time to time. Seems she travels with a faster crowd than her hubby and likes to throw his money around. We had a picture of her a couple of weeks ago, at some art opening, in a slinky white number with a double dip neckline. Nice build. Name's Marion."

● ● ●

Mrs. Wilcox, my cleaning lady, was due at one thirty, so I took the afternoon off and went to see *The Producers* for the second time. Came out humming "Springtime for Hitler," and hummed it all the way to my apartment on West 12th Street, then took a shower, and wasted some time choosing between the suit and the sport coat. I decided on the sport coat. I tucked the stub of a joint into my wallet for emergencies, rode an 8th Avenue local up to the Museum of Natural History, then walked a couple of blocks south to the Altamont Towers. If you fancied living on Central Park West, but didn't want to associate with the showbiz trash that infested the Dakota, the Altamont was for you. There were a few professional suites leased to high-end shrinks and dermatologists. The rest of the building was occupied by well-heeled families with tasteful summer homes in potato fields off the Montauk Highway—not too vulgarly close to the beach—and kids at Dalton and Riverdale.

The doorman didn't like me. I could tell by the way he checked out my hair. Its length was modest by the standards of the Electric Circus or Filmore East, but to a doorman at the Altamont Towers I looked like Mick Jagger, or maybe Janis Joplin. He stopped just short of patting me down, reluctantly consented to announce me, then summoned a flunky in a red vest, who had been polishing the brass fittings in the lobby, and instructed him to take me up to Mr. Kravitz's penthouse. This kid, who exuded all the charm of a dented spittoon, led me to an elevator that carried me to the floor marked P1. He let me out into a short corridor with a sinister Rothko on one wall and a single door.

As the elevator closed behind me, a maid in uniform opened the door. I told her I was Alex Novalis. She asked me in and conducted me into a sitting room furnished with an eclectic mixture of Empire gilt and ormolu and Milan midcentury modern. It was not what I had anticipated, and the same went for the art on the walls—a couple of late Picassos, a Braque papier collé, a Matisse from his cute-girl-in-harem-pants-and-nothing-else period, but also a big Lichtenstein Ben-Day dot panel, and a Jasper Johns flag. An inflated silver vinyl Warhol pillow floated against the ceiling near a gilded wood chandelier. There was no getting away from Andy that year.

The maid told me Mr. Kravitz would be with me in a few minutes, and asked if I would care for a Coke or some water while I was waiting. I asked for water. She disappeared, and I became aware of a woman sobbing. The sound was faint, and at first I thought that it might have been produced by a television in another room, but it soon became apparent that this was the real thing. A door opened, and a woman in a nurse's uniform appeared, carrying a towel. The sobbing became louder for a few seconds, as the nurse saw me and hesitated before closing the door behind her. She said, "Excuse me," and hurried off in the direction in which the maid had disappeared. Seconds later, the maid reappeared with my water.

I asked if everything was all right.

"I'm sorry, sir," she said in a lightly accented voice, "I don't understand."

Since that got me nowhere, I asked if I could use a bathroom.

Bathrooms are inordinately important to the rich. That's why they have so many in their homes. They are shrines where body and soul can be purged after a hard day of arbitrage, or strategic downsizing.

The one I was directed to was an expensively retrofitted example of the haute CPW genre. The designer had had the good taste to retain the tiny hexagonal floor tiles that can be found in many New York mansion blocks of a certain age. The furnishings, however, were somewhat more recent. The lavatory was truly a throne, its bowl and cistern encased in creamy porcelain. It was complemented by a matching washbasin and bidet, both sporting gold fittings. Most remarkable, though, was a shower cabinet enclosed in frosted glass. It served as a screen onto which were rear-projected schools of fish scudding about in some blue lagoon. As best I could tell, this projection had somehow been triggered as I entered. Now, as I approached the shower to get a better look, a panel of the glass screen began to glide silently open. This, I told myself, was a trip. Apparently, I had interrupted some photoelectric beam that instigated this magic. There, before me, was another set of gold handles. The temptation was impossible to resist. I reached out and gave the nearest one a gentle tug. A trickle of water splashed down from the showerhead, and with it came a cockroach of suitably majestic proportions. Upon hitting the marble floor of the shower, it gathered itself together with great dignity, and scuttled to the drain into which it disappeared.

● ● ●

When I got back to the sitting room, Gabriel Kravitz was waiting for me. He was a tall man, about fifty years old, lean and handsome in a Henry Fonda-ish kind of way, with a full head of graying hair, and the eyes of someone who was not accustomed to taking no for an answer. He wore a business suit that said, "I travel first class—got any problem with that?" and he was glaring at his watch. I had the impression that it was accustomed to being glared at. In his right hand he was holding a lowball glass heavy enough to work out with and containing something that might have been an old-fashioned. He didn't ask me to join him in whatever it was he was drinking, just waved for me to sit down, and took a seat himself. The sobbing continued in the background, but it didn't get billing.

"I'd like to see your license," he said.

I took it out of my pocket and handed it to him. He glanced at it and passed it back.

"How come they granted you a license after your conviction?"

"The charge was reduced to a misdemeanor. I took the test, I paid the fee, and anyway, I have connections."

I got the impression he liked at least the last part of that answer. He lit the first of the Marlboros that he would chain-smoke over the next hour or so.

"And what kind of cases do you specialize in?" he asked.

"Cases that involve art world fraud are my field of expertise."

"But you take what you can get—marital cases, missing persons..."

He'd done his research.

"What I've asked you here to talk about," said Kravitz, "involves the art world, but not art world fraud—at least not in the sense you're employing the term. It does, however, involve a missing person. Does the name Jerry Pedrosian mean anything to you?"

"He once threatened to throw me down a flight of stairs, but I didn't take it personally. He talks that way to everybody."

"So I've heard. Yet he seems to be highly regarded in some quarters."

"As an artist? Some people used to think he was the hottest thing since painting by numbers, but his reputation has been slipping lately. I don't think he sells much these days, though he's probably made enough to be comfortable."

"I gather you're not impressed?"

"I'm not paid to be a critic."

"But since you seem to know a good deal about art and the art market, you must have an opinion."

I thought about it for a second or two, not wanting to say anything too nice.

"As a painter, Jerry Pedrosian has some modest talent. When it comes to chutzpah, he's a genius. The best things he ever did were his happenings. Do you know about happenings? They're events staged as works of art. People like Allan Kaprow and Red Grooms, Jim Dine, and Claes Oldenburg—Pedrosian, too—would invite an audience and put on a show. But it wouldn't be like Judy Garland and Mickey Rooney on a soundstage at MGM. No straw skimmers and cute musical numbers. One of Pedrosian's happenings involved the audience being taken into an industrial refrigerator hung with sides of beef, while a girl in leathers revved the engine of a Harley till the noise was deafening. Not your cup of poison, maybe, but Pedrosian is a showman and knows how to sell that kind of thing."

Kravitz nodded, apparently unimpressed. He took a sip of his drink and paused, as if listening to something. The sobbing, perhaps.

"I'm not the collector in this family," he said. "I did buy the Matisse that's behind you—the girl with the vase of flowers—which is rather attractive, I think. Otherwise, my wife is responsible for what you see on the walls."

"She has a good eye. Or good advice."

"A good eye? Maybe. Nevertheless, she did buy several Pedrosian paintings some years ago, when he first attracted attention. We no longer own them. They were destroyed on my orders. I enjoyed watching them burn. To be blunt, though, I would have taken more pleasure in witnessing Jerry Pedrosian's destruction."

For a moment I thought he was trying to hire me as a hit man.

"Jerry Pedrosian," he continued, "seduced my daughter."

So that was the story.

"He has a reputation with women," I said.

"My daughter is not a woman," said Kravitz. "She is an eighteen-year-old girl. A freshman in college. Do you have any idea of Pedrosian's age? He's forty-three years old. He has a wife and four children."

"He hasn't lived with his wife in years. She took the kids to Oregon or someplace damp and depressing. I heard they were divorced."

"Is that supposed to make me feel better? Would you be happy to have your daughter involved with someone like Pedrosian?"

I assured him that I understood where he was coming from, and asked how this situation had come about.

"Lydia attends a college called Teddington, in Vermont. Perhaps you know of it? It's celebrated, it seems, for its encouragement of culturally adventurous activities. Lydia's mother thought it would suit her sensibility. I would have preferred somewhere with a more rounded curriculum. The girl's grades were good enough to get her into Radcliffe or Vassar or almost anywhere, but uncharacteristically, I caved in. I'm perhaps too fond of my daughter, and it was what she wanted. Teddington is an all-girls' school. She had gone to an all-girls' high school, Crufts, which, on the whole, had been a good choice. What could go wrong at an all-girls' college? What could go wrong is that the faculty would invite scum like Pedrosian up there to conduct so-called

9

experimental workshops. That was early in her first semester. I don't know exactly what happened, or when, but Lydia started coming down to the city rather often, though we rarely saw her when she was here. She said she was conducting social experiments, but as far as I can gather, she was hanging out at so-called artists' bars. Evidently, she was in contact with Pedrosian. She was sleeping with him. I suppose that was one of the social experiments."

"When was her eighteenth birthday?" I asked.

"The week she enrolled at Teddington."

"So, before she met Pedrosian?"

"Presumably."

"So there's not much that you can do about the situation, unless you hire a couple of guys from Newark to break his knees."

"It's crossed my mind," he said, "and it may yet come to that."

I asked him how he had found out about the affair.

"From her friend Andrea Marshall. A lovely girl. They've been best friends since kindergarten. Lydia tried to persuade Andrea to apply to Teddington. Luckily for Andrea's parents she chose NYU. She has a nice little place in the Village—on 10th Street."

I made a mental note of that. Not just a place in the Village. A *nice little* place in the Village.

"Let me get this straight," I said. "Lydia's best friend told you that Lydia's having an affair with a forty-three-year-old lothario? That doesn't sound like any best friend I ever heard of."

"Andrea opened up to me because she trusts me and because Lydia has disappeared. She's as worried as I am. Lydia came to town last weekend. She stopped here to drop off her bag. I wasn't home and didn't speak to her, but she told her mother that she was going downtown to what she described as a loft party on the Bowery. The Bowery, I ask you! They had a fight about it.

Lydia actually struck her mother. Unbelievable! She said she'd be meeting Andrea at this party and sleeping over at her apartment, but Andrea says she never heard of any such event—didn't even know Lydia was in town. Lydia left here in a huff, taking her bag with her. That was the last time anyone saw her. She didn't return to school. None of her friends have heard from her, or so they claim. More disturbing still, no one seems to know where Pedrosian is. I confronted his dealer, a man named Gruen—"

"Norbert Gruen. I know him."

"Who says that he believes Pedrosian has taken off on a cross-country car trip. Maybe headed for San Francisco, maybe for Los Angeles. No timetable, no route—a hippie odyssey. He may be stopping off in Chicago, or Denver. For all anyone knows, he may be joining one of those communes one reads about."

"Not Pedrosian's style. Whatever he is, he's not a hippie. He's been around too long to buy into that adolescent crap."

"In any case, Lydia is presumably with him."

"Or not."

"Whatever. I want to know where she is, and I'm certain this man is at the root of her disappearance. I don't want to go to the police—at least, not yet. And you'll understand, I'm sure, that I don't want the papers to get hold of the story. Are you prepared to take on the assignment of finding her and bringing her home—discreetly?"

"And what if she doesn't want to come home? She's eighteen years old. She can do what she likes."

"You just find her. Leave that part to me."

"And what if she's in real trouble?"

"We'll deal with that at the appropriate time."

●　●　●

Kravitz finally offered me a drink, and we spent some time discussing terms of employment and going over a list of names of Lydia's friends and other contacts that might be useful to me. Kravitz gave me a couple of photographs of his daughter. They showed a pretty, shy-looking girl, with straight blond hair, who looked younger than eighteen, and frighteningly innocent.

Before I left, I asked one final question.

"Would it be possible to talk to your wife while I'm here?"

"Are you deaf?" he said.

As he showed me out to the elevator, the sobbing continued.

TWO

By the time I got back downtown, it was getting dark.
I made my way to Max's Kansas City, the place where Jerry
Pedrosian was most likely to be found if he was in the city.
Located on a stretch of Park Avenue South where cab drivers
parked and took naps, Max's was the ultimate artists' bar, a spot
that had been colonized by the Warhol crowd. For that reason, it
also attracted would-be superstars, run-of-the mill drag queens,
poètes maudits, slumming society matrons hoping to catch a
glimpse of Candy Darling, and hipper members of the showbiz
crowd. You could even see a few politicos of liberal persuasion
who weren't shocked by the aroma of cannabis, or by an encounter with someone dressed for an S&M séance snorting coke in the
men's room. There were cheap red tablecloths on tables packed
together like cans of Spam on a shelf at D'Agostino's, but the art on
the walls was as good as you'd see in any New York gallery. Artists
like Bob Rauschenberg, John Chamberlain, and Dan Flavin had
bartered with Mickey Ruskin, the owner, trading work in return
for free food and bar tabs. Not that the food cost an arm and a leg
to begin with. A steak dinner would set you back $3.25 and came

with free chickpeas, or you could have a burger and fries for $1.10. Max's was a place to see and be seen, and that went equally for the celebrities and the miniskirted waitresses who were part of the show. The jukebox was deafeningly loud and the house wine was crap, but no one complained. Not even the Duke and Duchess of Windsor, who, on at least one occasion, had been seen there in all their frozen splendor.

It was early for Max's on a weeknight, and the place was only half full. I asked Sharon, who was working the door—keeping out undesirables—if she'd seen Jerry Pedrosian. Not for a few nights, she said. Mickey Ruskin was standing nearby, so I asked him the same question. Not since the weekend, he told me. I bought a drink and made my way to a booth near the bar, where one of the occupants was Doug Mills, a sculptor who had a studio a couple of buildings from Pedrosian on West Broadway.

"Have you seen Pedrosian lately?" I asked.

"That asshole?" said Mills. "I stay clear."

"I heard he might be away on a road trip."

"Not unless he's driving a rental car," said Mills. "That big ol' red Pontiac of his is parked in the lot next to the bodega. I saw it when I stopped there for cigarettes a couple of hours ago, right up against the chain-link fence where it usually is."

I quizzed a few more people, but all that I came up with was that Pedrosian had been at an opening at the Castelli Gallery several days earlier. He had been with a girl, but no one seemed to know who she was, though the general description fit Lydia Kravitz. There was no point hanging around, so I went to the phone booth near the kitchen and dialed the number I had been given for Lydia's girlfriend Andrea.

She picked up. I told her who I was and she said she'd been expecting to hear from me.

"Lydia's dad called me an hour ago."

I asked if I could stop by to see her. She said she'd rather meet somewhere more neutral, and we settled on the little triangular park—not much more than a traffic island with a couple of undernourished trees—where Bleecker Street intersects with 6th Avenue and Downing Street. I told her I'd be reading the *Voice*. I got there early and sat on the only bench that wasn't occupied by elderly Italian women in widows' weeds. The girl was fifteen minutes late. I don't know why, but I was expecting a Haight-Ashbury waif—granny glasses and an ankle-length flower-power dress. Andrea Marshall didn't fit that stereotype at all. If Lydia Kravitz, in her photographs at least, appeared the epitome of innocence, her best friend gave off a very different vibe. She was about five five and verged on the voluptuous, with short, sculpted, dark hair—*École de Vidal Sassoon*—white skin, and big chestnut-colored eyes. She wore a denim miniskirt, a white T-shirt with no bra underneath, and white vinyl boots. I would have paid attention even if she hadn't had been carrying a Bloomingdale's shopping bag with a gun in it.

It was a medium-caliber automatic, loosely wrapped in tissue paper. She opened the bag to show it to me. I told her to keep it out of sight for Christ's sake, and ordered her to follow me.

We walked south on the west side of 6th Avenue, away from the Village action, and into a zone that was pretty quiet after dark. As soon as I thought it was safe to talk, I asked her where she'd got the damn thing.

"It was in Lydia's overnight bag."

"And Lydia left the bag with you?"

Andrea nodded.

"I thought you didn't see her last weekend?"

"That's what I told her dad."

"Why?"

"I was scared, and her dad can be creepy. I didn't want to get Lydia into trouble."

"Creepy? Gabriel Kravitz seems to think you're the cat's pajamas," I said.

"I know," she said. "I told you he was creepy."

I thought of the way Kravitz had spoken of Andrea's "nice little place in the Village."

"Has he ever been to your apartment?"

"Why would I let him come to my apartment?" she asked, apparently upset by the question.

"When I start out on an investigation like this," I told her, "a lot of things don't make sense, and I have to ask dumb questions to try to figure out what's going on. Let's try this—why did you tell Lydia's dad she was sleeping with Jerry Pedrosian? Weren't you afraid that that would get her into trouble?"

Patches of red appeared under her eyes.

"I thought he already knew."

"And why are you telling me now that you saw Lydia last weekend, when you told him you didn't know she'd been in town? You know I'm working for Mr. Kravitz. Surely you'd presume that I'm likely to go back to him and spill the beans?"

"Why am I telling you? Because I'm fucking scared!"

There was a long pause—tears glinted in Andrea's eyes—before she continued.

"Lydia had a fight with her mom and came down to my place. I said she could sleep over. We went to a party on the Bowery— the studio of some painter. Lydia got very nervous waiting for Jerry. She was sure he was going to stand her up. Are you going to tell Mr. Kravitz all this—about me seeing her?"

I ignored the question.

"You know Jerry Pedrosian?"

"I met him a couple of times. He didn't give me the time of day. Once I went to the movies with them. It was embarrassing. They were necking like they were alone somewhere. His hands were all over her. Everywhere. It was like I wasn't there."

Knowing Pedrosian, I would have guessed that Andrea was more his type—more available looking—but where Lydia was concerned I only had snapshots to go by.

"When Jerry finally showed up at the party that night," said Andrea, "Lydia got really upset because he ignored her and danced with another girl. Finally, he came over—barely looked at me, of course—and took Lydia away. And that was the last I saw of her."

"He took her away?"

"They danced for a while. It was a mob scene. Have you ever been to a loft party? Then I didn't see them again. I guess they just took off. I didn't think anything of it. That was kind of what I'd expected to happen. "

"That was the last time you saw her?"

Andrea nodded.

"So, when did you go through her bag?"

"Not till today, after her dad called."

"And what did you think when you found the gun?"

"What kind of question is that? I didn't know what to think. I was terrified."

She was getting very agitated.

"But you didn't tell her dad?"

"Obviously not, okay? And now you're going to ask me why not? I don't know, okay? I was just fucking scared. It isn't every day I find a gun in my best friend's bag. Then, when Lydia's dad called me again to say that he'd hired a private detective, I got scared all over again and I thought maybe I'd better give you the real story. Are you going to tell him?"

In a fraction of a second, she had gone from confrontational to contrite and vulnerable, which made her seem much prettier.

I thought for a moment.

"No, not until I have to," I told her. "So long as you're honest with me, I'll try to keep things under wraps."

We were under a lamppost and she gave me a Little Girl Lost look. It was a look that probably worked pretty well on NYU boys majoring in English Lit. Come to think of it, I always wanted to write a dissertation on the contemporary relevance of *The Scarlet Letter.*

"I haven't eaten," she said.

That was to the point. I took her to a little Italian place on MacDougal, and watched as she scarfed down a man-sized portion of spaghetti puttanesca, washed down with something the owner passed off as chianti. Meanwhile, I tried to figure out what I'd got myself into. Common sense told me I should head directly to the 6th Precinct a few blocks away, hand over the gun, and tell the cops the whole story. Maybe I should call Kravitz first, but either way, he wasn't going to like the cops getting involved since that almost guaranteed that the press would have the story. Then there was Andrea to think about.

But why did I give a damn about Andrea? She meant nothing to me, but she was one of those girls who get under your skin from the moment you set eyes on them. I guess she brought out my fraternal instincts.

I told her to sit tight while I took the Bloomingdale's bag with the automatic in it to the men's room. My regular line of work sometimes involves inspecting delicate prints and drawings that can be compromised by greasy fingerprints, so I always carry a couple of pairs of cotton gloves for emergencies. I slipped a pair on and inspected the little pistol. It was a compact .38-caliber semiautomatic—a Ruger, the kind of lightweight pistol law enforcement officers sometimes carried as backup weapons, and that bad guys liked because they're small and easily concealed. It held a full magazine, but as far as I could tell—firearms forensics is not my field—it had not been fired recently. The bag also had an ankle holster to fit the gun.

I sat on the toilet, staring at a chromolithograph of Monte Pellegrino and wondering what to do next. A cool head is useful in these situations, and for once, I made the smart decision. I would call Kravitz, tell him this was a police matter, then march over to the 6th Precinct with both Andrea and the gun. Kravitz wouldn't like it, and neither would Andrea, but tough shit.

There was a snag. When I left the toilet, Andrea was nowhere to be seen.

I asked the guido behind the counter where she was. He grinned and jerked a thumb toward the door.

"Looks like she bailed on you, pal."

"She just walked out?"

"Soon as you went to the bathroom, a guy showed up in the doorway and she took off with him."

"What kind of a guy?"

"A fuckin' guy, okay? Nobody told me shit to check out what kind of fuckin' guy. Not big, not fuckin' small, A kid in jeans and a T-shirt—long fuckin' hair, a Mets cap, and a gray fuckin' T-shirt that said property of something or other…"

"Did he force her to go with him?"

The guido shrugged.

"He just gave her a fuckin' nod and she went."

"She didn't say anything?"

"Yeah—she said you'd take care of the fuckin' check."

THREE

It was a good bet that the dude Andrea had taken off with had been shading us the whole time, and that she knew it all along. Maybe just a boyfriend she'd asked to keep an eye on things. Or maybe something else. My immediate plan was to get the gun to my office, where there was a safe, but since there was a significant possibility that somebody might still be following me, I decided to play the private-eye game. I took a subway to Times Square, changing cars a couple of times, bought a ticket for a movie called *Bikers in Bikinis*, sat through half a reel of soft-core sleaze, then exited through a side door and took a cab to Union Square. The night doorman on duty was Walter, who had once been a porter on the Pennsylvania Railroad. He told me that someone had been there looking for me about an hour earlier.

"Pretty little white girl. She seemed upset about something. Kinda nervous."

"Did she give a name?"

Walter shook his head. I took out the snapshots of Lydia.

"Is this her?"

"Sure could be her. Yeah, I guess so. Maybe…"

"Did she leave any message? Say how I could reach her?"

"No. I just told her you're not here at this time of night and she went away. Was that okay, chief? If I knew you'd be here tonight..."

I thanked Walter and took the elevator up to my floor. There was a light showing under the door of my office. I was pretty sure I hadn't left it on—it's the kind of thing I'm anal about. I stared at it for a while. The light under the door was mocking me. "You've seen too many B movies," it said. "You're getting paranoid. Too much of that righteous Costa Rican shit. There's no one in there, no one pressed up against the wall, holding his breath with a big blue gun held flat against the lapels of a double-breasted suit, ready to crack the muzzle down against the back of your skull the moment you open the door. And anyway, you've got a piece, too, snug in that nice Bloomie's bag you're carrying. If you feel nervous—and maybe you should—put on those fancy cotton gloves, take the pretty little heater out of the bag, and come on in..."

It hit me that I was going a little bit crazy, but that can happen when you're a couple of hours into a missing persons investigation and you find yourself in possession of someone else's fully loaded automatic. That wasn't supposed to happen in the kind of cases I got involved in. Things like that can change the way you think about little surprises like a light under a door.

Then I remembered. Mrs. Wilcox, the cleaning lady, had been there that afternoon. Mystery solved.

Just for the hell of it, though, I kicked the door open. I don't know what I expected to achieve by that, but it was something I'd wanted to do ever since I'd seen Victor Mature do it in some black-and-white flick when I was a kid. The room was empty except for the ghosts of all the losers who had occupied it before me. I opened the wall safe, which, like all good wall safes, was hidden behind a painting—a framed reproduction of Edward

Hopper's *Office at Night*—and deposited the gun and the holster there. They joined my emergency money, a few contracts, and some personal papers. I closed the safe, scrambled the combination, then sat down at my desk to check my messages on the brand new Ansaphone my ex-wife had given me for my birthday.

The first message was from her. She said she was feeling sad. The second was from T & G Air-Conditioning, a company I had placed a call to earlier in the day. The third was from Gimbels, my department store of choice, reminding me that my monthly ounce of flesh was two months overdue. The last one was more interesting. I heard the machine pick up, but there was nothing else except the sound of breathing and a sigh of frustration that was unmistakably female.

Lydia?

It was still only ten thirty and I was in no mood to go home and watch Johnny Carson. I could stroll back to Max's, have a drink, and see if anyone had shown up who might have a lead on Pedrosian. Or I could check out Andrea's apartment, though after the way she'd behaved, it seemed unlikely that she'd be hanging out anywhere I could track her down. Or I could head down to SoHo where Pedrosian had his loft.

I grabbed the phone book and looked up his number. He was unlisted. As I sat there, turning over the possibilities, I reached into my pocket for my last Gauloise—a nouvelle vague affectation of mine—crumpled the package, and tossed it into the wastebasket under my desk. It was half full. Then I noticed that there was still ash in the ashtray, and the things on my desk top—the Selectric, the yellow pads, the HB pencils, the Mont Blanc pen, the bronze souvenir of the Perisphere and Trylon from the 1939 World's Fair—had not been straightened out. When I checked further, the windowsill was covered in a film of New York soot you could write your name in. Mrs. Wilcox had been a no-show.

There was nothing especially unusual in this since she was given to taking days off without remembering to let me know, but then what explained the fact that the lights had been left on?

I told myself I was definitely getting paranoid, and decided to pay Pedrosian's neighborhood a visit.

● ● ●

SoHo, in those days, was just a godforsaken industrial ghetto wedged between Little Italy and Even Littler Italy. It didn't have a proper name. Firemen called it Hell's Hundred Acres because so many of them had been killed or maimed in fires there. Other people called it the loft district and left it at that because that's what it was—two dozen square blocks of Victorian loft buildings that, until a few years earlier, had been packed with sweatshops and other shabby businesses scavenging at the low end of the commercial food chain—manufacturers of novelties and cheap jewelry, dealers in rags and scrap metal. Sure, the buildings were of enormous historical importance, masterpieces of cast iron, and part of New York's cultural heritage, but who knew? They'd been neglected for decades, were coated in grime, and pissed on by dogs and bums, and by Robert Moses who wanted to tear half of them down to make way for a ten-lane elevated expressway. In 1968, a few businesses that had been there for decades still held on. Others had moved out to New Jersey or North Carolina, or wherever the cheap labor was. As lofts became vacant and rents plunged, artists had begun to move in, thrilled to find fifteen-hundred square feet of raw space for a hundred and fifty bucks a month.

I walked south to the intersection of Prince and Mercer, to Fanelli's, a comfy tavern used by both artists and working stiffs. In those days, Mike Fanelli, who'd run the place since Prohibition, closed up when he felt like it, and tonight was one of the nights he'd gone home early. So I headed west on Prince to a Mafioso bar, on the far side of West Broadway, where loft dwellers sometimes stopped by to shoot pool in the back room. It was almost empty, but at a corner table Martin Wolfe was bullshitting two girls in tie-dye T-shirts and a young dude with a beret, a mustache, and serious sideburns. Probably students from Cooper Union or SVA—at least, they had paint on their jeans. Wolfe had paint on his jeans, too, and his share of facial hair, but his beard was getting grizzled, though he was probably still in his forties. He had been one of those talented younger painters—along with the likes of Mike Goldberg, Alfred Leslie, and Friedel Dzubas—who had toiled in the shadows of giants like Pollock and de Kooning, hanging out with the masters at the Eighth Street Club and the Cedar Tavern. He'd learned from the best, and that went for his expansive and disputatious manner as well as his work.

I heard him before I even saw him, a pastrami sandwich of a voice, cured with plenty of garlic somewhere in the shtetels that once clustered around the Grand Concourse.

"You kids think you're hot shit. You go on a couple of marches to protest the war—smoke a joint, hug the Washington Monument, get laid by someone with an Afro, sing a few choruses of 'We Shall Overcome'—and you think you're fuckin' Che Guevara on roller skates. You've seen it all, you've got all the answers."

"That's not what I'm saying," the boy with the sideburns protested angrily, his accent from somewhere west of the rust belt. "What I *am* saying is that, as artists, we have the possibility—the duty—to reimagine the political landscape."

"*Aspiring* artists," Wolfe corrected him. "And what is this political landscape going to look like? Billboards of Mao along every interstate? Fidel added to Mount Rushmore?"

"I mean," said the boy, flushed with self-righteousness, "that we've got to rethink everything. Start from scratch, man."

"Let me give you one bit of advice," said Wolfe. "If you become an artist—and I hope you make it—don't forget that you're still going to be a worker. Nothing more, nothing less. You'll get plenty of practice, because if you do make it, you're going to drive a fucking cab first, or serve tables, or learn to put up drywall—"

"I can already put up drywall," said the kid huffily.

"Then you're on your way," said Wolfe. "But what I'm trying to tell you is that your paintings may hang on the walls of the Museum of Modern Art, you may be feasted by Wall Street princelings, and feted by titans of the military-industrial complex, but it doesn't mean shit. Whatever happens, you're still working for the Man. He may pay thousands of bucks for your paintings, and tell you you're the greatest genius to grow his hair long since Leonardo da Vinci, but you're still down there with the paid help, just like the butler, the caddy, the family attorney, the crooked accountant, the hooker, and the fag decorator."

The kid was about to respond, but Wolfe had spotted me and his face lit up.

"My friend is here," he said. "I gotta go."

With that, he stood up, telling the kid, "Keep the faith, baby," then grabbed me by the arm, and led me toward the exit.

"I hope you didn't plan a rendezvous with some hot bimbo in here," he said, "because I've gotta get away from these kids before they drive me crazy. Come back to my place, and I'll buy you a drink."

Martin Wolfe and I knew each other pretty well, though our relationship hadn't always been as relaxed as it was now. The biggest case I had been involved with during my sojourn at the DA's office had been what one newspaper had dubbed The

Factory of Fabulous Fakes. A Dutchman named Smit, himself a talented forger, had set up a stable of forgers, each specializing in the work of one or two artists. Wolfe, whose own paintings were not selling at the time, had linked up with Smit and proved extremely adept at faking the work of Marc Chagall. To this day, there are probably dozens of canvases titled *Clown with Mandolin* or *Village with Two Lovers and Donkey in Opera Hat* hanging in distinguished public and private collections around the world, purporting to be Chagalls, but, in fact, painted by Marty Wolfe, who had become a key figure in the investigation. I had been instrumental in negotiating a plea bargain that enabled him to escape with a suspended sentence in return for the evidence he supplied against Smit. The story was commonly known in the art world, but it had only served to enhance Wolfe's reputation, making his own work moderately sought after once more. He was the kind of guy who knew a lot of people and heard about a lot of things, so I took him up on his invitation.

We walked the short distance to his building on Grand Street, skirting bales of rags, watching the rats party in the gutter, not encountering a soul. Wolfe's current modest success was evident in the furnishings of his loft. In those days, most lofts occupied by artists were raw spaces tarted up with the basic amenities—self-installed plumbing, a camp bed, a worktable, and a few chairs scavenged from the street. In addition to studio space, Wolfe's loft had a fully equipped bathroom, a partitioned-off bedroom, an open kitchen built around a butcher-block island, and polyurethane floors. Throw in a couple of matched Borzois and it would have been camera-ready for *Architectural Digest*.

He poured me a scotch, mixed a vodka tonic for himself, and showed me some new paintings he was working on. I cut through the small talk and asked him if he'd run into Pedrosian lately.

"I saw him in the liquor store on Canal Street a few days ago. He was cashing a check."

"How long ago?"

"Friday, maybe?" Wolfe shrugged.

"How big a check?"

"I've no idea. I don't know how much credit Manny allows him."

"Did he say anything about going out of town?"

"No. He asked me about Pol Smit. He said he'd heard that Pol's been sick. I told him he's been diagnosed with cancer."

"Why was he interested?" I asked.

Wolfe grinned.

"That's right," he said, "I forgot that even you don't know about that, but you had your suspicions, I remember. I guess it's okay now that it's all done with, and you're not the Man anymore. Let me put it this way—and you didn't hear this from me—there was someone who looked a lot like Pedrosian who was in on the game with Smit, but who managed to stay clean when the shit hit the fan. This guy had an unusual specialty. Collage. You don't hear much about people who do fake collages, but this guy had a real feel for it. He could do you a Kurt Schwitters even a specialist would swear was the real thing—Max Ernst, Picasso—he really knew how to pull that stuff off."

When I had been investigating the Smit case, I had had my suspicions that Pedrosian might have been involved, but I'd never come up with anything that linked him to Smit. Now I remembered that back in one of his early shows, Pedrosian had shown a group of collages montaged from magazine clippings and technical drawings torn out from some old textbook. I recalled that, at the time, I had thought that he had a nice touch.

"That's not why you're asking about him, though—I hope," said Wolfe, looking a little uncomfortable, "because, like I said, you didn't hear anything from me."

"Nothing to do with any of that," I assured him, "but I could use his phone number if you have it."

Wolfe wrote something on a scrap of paper and handed it to me.

"We used to hang out back then," he said, grinning. "We used to kid ourselves that producing fakes was an antibourgeois gesture—a critique of the underlying values of capitalism. Jerry's come a long way since then."

FOUR

In those days, someone with my modest income could afford to rent the parlor floor of a row house in the West Village. Mine was on West 12th, between Hudson Street and the Hudson River. At about one thirty that morning, there was a knock on the window. I knew who it was. Janice, my ex. She made a habit of doing this. I got out of bed, let her in, and asked her if she could use a drink. She shook her head.

"I'm already sad," she said.

She sat down on the worn leather sofa I had inherited with the apartment and looked up at me with a wan smile. Samba, the cat I had inherited with the sofa, jumped up beside her and stretched onto her lap. Samba liked Janice. Maybe she reminded him of the whores in the Sao Paolo bordello where he'd been raised, but that's not only a different story, it's an entirely different genre.

"Where's the boyfriend?" I asked.

"LA," said Janice. "He's shooting a pilot. I don't know if he'll be back."

"I thought this was the real thing."

"As real as it gets with an actor."

"So what can I do for you?"

"I don't want to sleep alone. Is that okay?"

This was a familiar routine, repeated a couple of times a month. We had it down pat.

"Yeah, that's okay."

I sat on the edge of the bed and smoked the tail end of a joint as I watched her undress. Her body still interested me. I guess she knew it because she took her time and occasionally glanced over to make sure I was watching.

"So you still sleep with your watch on," she said.

"Why would I change?"

"Did I ever tell you it bothered me?"

"About a million times."

"It always seemed to mean that you weren't fully committed— a part of your head was somewhere else. You know what I mean?"

She was down to her underwear by now, an image spoiled only by the prehistoric pantyhose women wore in the sixties, which never quite fit and always seemed to be baggy around the crotch.

"Take it off," she said. "Just this once. For me. Let yourself be completely naked."

I took the watch off and put it on the night table.

She mimed applause, removed the offending tights, and climbed into bed. I took a couple more drags and climbed in with her. She turned her back.

"It's been a long day," she said.

"I guess so," I said, easing up to her.

"Thanks for being here for me," she said. "It must be difficult, you knowing I've been sleeping with other men."

"I'll get used to it," I told her.

She giggled.

"It probably turns you on."

"Hey," I said, "none of my business. We're both single."

"Feels like you're making it your business," she said.

My erection was pressed up against her ass.

"Trouble is my business," I said.

"Come on," she said. "Sometimes you've got to think about me fucking other men. It's only natural."

This was part of the routine we went through every time she stopped by.

"Sometimes I do," I said. "Did you ever sleep with Jerry Pedrosian?"

Janice sat up in bed, as if I stuck a needle into her.

"How did you know about that?" she demanded.

I was taken aback by her reaction.

"I didn't," I said.

"Because I know I never told you about him," she said. "That was when we were still together. While you were on that junket to Mexico—something to do with a Poussin ripped off by the Nazis."

And I had to ask!

● ● ●

The phone woke me at seven thirty. It was Kravitz. He wanted to know if I had made any progress. I gave him a rundown on my previous evening, acknowledging meeting with Andrea, but leaving out most of what she'd told me, and any mention of the gun. I made it sound as much like a bland police report as I could manage.

"Sounds like you found out exactly what I already knew," he said, hanging up on me.

Janice looked tasty, sprawled out on my bed, half-covered by a sheet, but I dressed and got out of there, bought a *New York Times*, and ate breakfast in a greasy spoon on 8th Avenue. I learned that American troops had suffered heavy losses during a firefight in Quang Tri Province, the Russians had conducted an underground nuclear test, the Beatles had opened a new Apple boutique somewhere in Blighty, and Bruno the hyperactive short-order cook had had a falling out with his mother-in-law. Business as usual.

I headed east on 14th Street, past the Puerto Rican stores selling transistor radios, Julio Iglesias records, and communion dresses. It was already warming up, and ominous-looking clouds were massing behind me. By the time I reached Union Square, the place was jumping, crowds headed for the subway entrances. The usual group of lushes was parked alongside the Temperance fountain, and a skinny black kid dressed as Mahatma Gandhi harangued commuters with a speech that no one paid any attention to.

I bought a coffee from the Dominican guy at the kiosk on the corner of 16th Street and took it up to my office. I checked the safe. Not that I thought that the gun would have disappeared, but I checked it anyway. Then I checked my answering machine. No new messages. I remembered that Wolfe had written down how to reach Pedrosian's number. He was listed as Michigan J. Frog. It was a big thing in New York at the time. Artists who fancied they were about to become world famous had themselves listed under fictitious monikers. It was like wearing shades in the hope of passing as a movie star. Andy had started the whole thing. He was listed as Clark Kent. Everyone aped Andy. Pedrosian's choice was the Tin Pan Alley star of a classic Chuck Jones cartoon.

I grabbed the phone book, looked up Michigan J. Frog, and dialed. Pedrosian had an Ansaphone, too. It broadcast a few bars of "The Michigan Rag" then announced, "You have reached the studio of Michigan J. Frog. Please leave a message after the tone."

I hung up and tried to think of something clever to do next. That's when the door was pushed open, and in walked Mrs. Gabriel Kravitz. She wasn't what I'd pictured, but it had to be her.

She was still a good-looking woman with an enviable figure, but there wasn't much left of the former Miss Cuyahoga County. It wasn't hard to picture her in a one-piece swimsuit, but it was tough to imagine this piece of work as a kid facing a panel of Cleveland car dealers and greasy-haired dance academy impresarios, spouting her piece about the wholesomeness of the American family. As for what her talent was, back in the Truman era, I wouldn't care to guess. In any case, she had shampooed all trace of the industrial hinterlands out of her Grace Kelly hair and transformed herself into a million-dollar Manhattan matron.

She was done up in a tailored linen safari suit, from the souks of Saks Fifth Avenue. On her head was a safari hat with a floppy brim that shaded her eyes, which were already concealed behind oversize Ray-Bans, ideal for hiding any telltale signs of recent tears. Everything about her appearance signaled concealment, yet at the same time invited you to imagine what was underneath. The outfit verged on the severe, but when she moved, the way the skirt moved led you to believe you would not be disappointed by her legs, or anything adjacent.

Without introducing herself, she sat in the chair across the desk from me, and helped herself to one of my cigarettes.

"I quit last month," she explained.

Taking her time, she lit the Gauloise, inhaled, and looked around the office.

"I used to work in a place like this," she told me. "Seventy words per minute on an old Underwood, and my shorthand was not to be believed, darling. Spec*ta*cular. Sometimes I wish I was back there."

She didn't look or sound like someone who had spent much time behind a desk, unless it was the reception desk at some billion-dollar foundation—one of those volunteer jobs you segue into when you're the kind of girl who doesn't want to take a real job away from someone who needs it. Marion Kravitz had totally reinvented herself, down to the *Breakfast at Tiffany's* drawl.

"For lunch," she continued, "we'd go to this place called the Diamond Deli, on Main Street. That was in Akron, Ohio. Nobody in this town realizes that Akron is the *real* corned beef capital of America. You can have your Lower East Side, darling—there's nothing there to touch the Diamond Deli. Reubens to die for! And on Saturday nights I'd go to a movie at the Linda with Jimmy Stone—I liked the ones with hardboiled guys like Robert Mitchum and femmes fatales. Did you like femmes fatales, darling?"

I thought it was about time I got a word in, so, rather than answering, I asked, "Whatever happened to Jimmy Stone?"

"Poor Jimmy," she said, contemplating the glowing tip of the cigarette. "He joined the army. He said they would draft him anyway, so he signed up, and he was probably very good at being a soldier because he was very brave—quite stupid, really—and very well endowed. I can vouch for that. He wanted me to marry him, poor darling, but I didn't fancy that sort of life—would you? Shopping for diapers at the PX, nights out in downtown Wiesbaden with the warrant officers' wives...Anyway, they sent Jimmy to Korea. He stepped on a landmine and his balls were blown off. A loss to womankind. By then, I'd moved on. I got a job in the big city—Cleveland—with a divinely boring insurance company. And I met a boy there who was frightfully clever at managing risk, if you know what I mean, and he said I should enter this beauty pageant. I told him not to be a silly, but he told me that, if I won, it would be *my* insurance policy. And— surprise, surprise—I did win, and because of that I met all kinds of interesting and unusual people. By unusual I mean people with unusual needs. And then I got married to Gabe and we moved to the Apple, though we still have a sweet little mansion in Shaker Heights. See, darling, now you know my entire life story."

She stubbed the cigarette out angrily in the ashtray and just sat there, staring at me through the Ray-Bans. I asked her to take them off.

"Screw you," she said.

I told her that when I'm talking to someone, I like to see their eyes. Otherwise, we might just as well talk on the phone.

"That's not a very nice thing to say to a lady," she said, smoothing her skirt.

"Do you wear them when you haven't been crying?" I asked.

"Only when I want to be invisible."

"That must be a tough trick to pull off."

"You do realize," she said, "that you're talking to the wife of your current employer?"

"I kind of thought so. It's fairly unusual for women who look like they stepped out of the social pages to drop by my office to tell me the story of their life. Even if they cut it short right after the interesting part about meeting people with unusual needs."

She took off the glasses and glared at me angrily.

"I presume you were trying to let me know you were one of the boys," I said. "Or should I say one of the girls? I don't know why, but I thought maybe that was your intention."

Her expression softened.

"I was nervous," she said. "I talk too much when I'm nervous."

Her eyes were rimmed with red, which expertly applied makeup had failed to hide.

"So, shall we start again?" I asked.

"My husband told me he'd hired you," she said. "I thought I'd look you over."

The affected delivery had vanished.

"Disappointed?"

"What I told you is true," she said. "I've done my turn in offices like this."

"But you were hoping for something fancier?"

"Don't put words into my mouth, Mr. Novalis. Knowing Gabe, I thought he'd hire someone with a cute secretary, a Brooks Brothers suit, and a shitload of certificates on the wall. I'm kind of pleasantly surprised."

"Maybe he wants to get the job done."

"Oh, he wants to get the job done. He wants to put Lydia back in the ivory tower he built for her, and have Jerry Pedrosian's balls on toast for breakfast. That's if I don't get to the bastard first."

"You know Pedrosian?" I prompted.

"I know the son of a bitch. I used to buy his paintings. That was when I thought he was an artist first and a rat second. Gabe tells me you know the bastard, too."

"We've crossed paths. What's your theory on what's going on between him and your daughter? I understand you saw her after she came down from Vermont."

"Yeah, I saw her. She was in one of her 'I must have been switched at birth because a wretch like you couldn't possibly be my mother' moods. Let's get one thing straight; Lydia isn't the virginal creature she appears to be and that her father likes to pretend she is. She was a sweet kid, once upon a time—and always the center of attention because she was impossibly cute—but when she hit about thirteen, everything changed. She became trouble with a capital *T*. The wrong crowd at school—including that parasite Andrea Marshall—problems with drugs, pregnant before her sixteenth birthday."

She stopped, obviously uncomfortable with what she'd blurted out.

"I shouldn't have said that," she said. "You never heard that—understand?"

People were always telling me I hadn't heard what they'd just told me.

"Her father doesn't know about all this?" I guessed out loud.

"Maybe you are the right guy for the job," said Mrs. Kravitz. "And maybe I should learn to keep my mouth shut."

"A little late for that."

She glared some more.

"But Lydia's smart," she went on. "Always got good grades, no matter what kind of mess she was in. She could have gone to school anywhere, but she insisted on going to Teddington."

"I thought that was your idea."

"Did he tell you that? He probably thinks it's true. I went along with the idea—that's the most I'll admit to."

"Why did she choose an all-girls' school? Doesn't sound like her kind of scene."

"Are you kidding? Girls' schools are magnets for boys— not to mention men who should be old enough to know better, including the half of the faculty that isn't queer. Anyway, Gabe has convinced himself that Lydia is Doris Day in an embryonic state. Sure, she's naughty once in a while, but only when she's been led astray, usually by Andrea Marshall, who also can do no wrong in my husband's eyes. That girl's been able to wrap him around her little finger ever since she began to sprout tits. Gabe knows everything there is to know about the construction industry, but he doesn't know shit about women, especially when they're nubile and hot to trot. Not that he'd ever touch one of those kids, mind you. He just wants to worship them from afar."

By now, Mrs. Kravitz had dropped her guard entirely. I mentioned that her husband had said that Lydia had told her she was planning to stay with Andrea.

"Who claims she never saw her, but the little bitch is as trustworthy as a Washington lawyer. Watch out for her, Mr. Novalis."

She put her Ray-Bans back on.

"What are you going to do next, darling?" she asked, resuming her affected uptown accent.

"I'll do what I usually do in a missing persons, case," I said, "except that your husband doesn't want me to go to the police."

"That's one thing on which we can agree," she said, standing up to leave.

"Is there a number where you can be reached?" I asked. "It might be better in certain circumstances if I didn't have to go through your husband."

She liked that.

"I run into a lot of certain circumstances," she said, giving me a phone number that I wrote down on a yellow pad. "That's my boudoir number," she said. "Use it sparingly, and please be careful."

"Careful of Pedrosian?" I asked.

"Him for starters," she said.

FIVE

I decided to head uptown to pay a visit to Norbert
Gruen, Pedrosian's dealer. As I walked across the park, toward
the subway, I had a sense that someone was watching me. You
know how it is when you're looking hard at someone in a crowd,
and suddenly that person can feel that you're eyeballing them
and turns to look at you? I had the feeling that that person gets,
and I had it strongly enough that I sat down on a bench to light
a cigarette I didn't need, in order to check out my surroundings.
There was no unusual action that I could see in my immediate
vicinity—a pair of mothers with baby carriages, a dog walker
with three Irish wolfhounds, a couple of elderly black guys playing checkers, several young women who might be students from
NYU or Parsons handing out leaflets touting Gene McCarthy for
President, a man in a dashiki, a couple of hard hats, some Puerto
Rican kids cutting school. I had been headed for the subway
entrance opposite S. Klein's department store, but now I changed
direction and headed toward the entrance at the southwest corner of the park. I still had a prickly feeling at the back of my neck,
as if I was being eyeballed. Maybe someone was watching me

from a window overlooking the park. When I went down into the subway, however, I still felt eyes stabbing me in the back, and they seemed to follow me as I walked along the busy concourse that connects the two BMT lines with the IRT Lexington Avenue Line, where I was headed. I paused again, pretending to check out a magazine at a newsstand. Nothing suspicious. Paranoia, I told myself, but the events of the last twenty-four hours continued to spook me.

I descended the stairs from the mezzanine level to the uptown platform. Morning rush hour was over, but the platform was fairly crowded. As an IRT express rattled around the curve, a tourist with a German accent waved a map in front of me and asked me how please to get to the Statue of Liberty? I was explaining that he needed a downtown train when—just as the express was about to pull level with me and commuters were pushing forward in anticipation—somebody gave me a hard shove from behind. I had been trying to communicate with the German by gesture, and the shove caught me off balance. I staggered forward and was about to fall onto the tracks. My fate flashed in front of me—decapitated by the flanged wheels of an Interborough train among discarded soft drink containers and candy wrappers, for the amusement of an audience of Norway rats, and possibly toasted at the same time. People screamed, and as I pitched forward, somebody grabbed my jacket. I felt a warm breath of air as the train whooshed inches past my nose, and saw wide-eyed faces staring at me from inside the cars. Then I was pulled back, jerked upright, and discovered that I'd been saved by a guy built like a sanitation truck, with eyes that were almost pink—like a rabbit's—a flat nose and frizzy hair.

"You wuz pushed," he said. "You wuz seriously pushed."

"Yeah," said someone else, and someone else, too, though most people were busy battling their way onto the train before the doors closed.

"Did you see him?" I asked.

"It was a her," said my savior. "Skinny, shoulder-length hair, blue jeans—those ones with the wide bottoms—dark T-shirt. She took off for the exit. I wudda stopped her, but then you'd be goulash, and everyone else would be late for work."

"It was a man," said a woman in a babushka. "I saw his Adam's apple. A man with red hair."

"Don't be crazy—it was a girl," said the man with the pink eyes.

"Anyway, it was an accident," said someone else.

"Then why did she run for it?"

"Because he was fuckin' scared. Because he thought that a bunch of crazies were goin' to say he did it."

"Fuckin' A she did it. That wuz a serious shove."

While they argued about this, I looked around for the German tourist, but he was nowhere to be seen. Had he been deliberately distracting me? Setting me up?

Two transit cops showed up and began asking questions. The whole routine was repeated. "It was a man..." "It was a girl..." "You can't tell the difference these days..." "Shoulder-length hair..." "Yeah, down to the shoulders..." "Red hair..." "I'd say more sort of medium brown..." "C'mon—she was blond..." "About thirty..." "No, she was about as old as my youngest daughter who is just pregnant with her first kid..."

And so on till everyone got bored. I thanked the man who had saved me, wrote down his name—Lech Zelenski—and phone number, and promised to take him and his wife out for a spaghetti dinner. He said, "Think nuthin' of it..."

Then the cops asked me to make a written statement, so I went back to their cubbyhole office up on the mezzanine and did as they asked. I told them it was probably an accident, though I didn't believe that for one moment. It didn't make much difference since they weren't about to launch a major investigation. Then I signed the paper and got up to leave.

The older cop, who had a mustache that would have earned him a part in a Mack Sennett two reeler, wagged a finger at me.

"Let that be a lesson," he said.

"A lesson in what?"

"Think about it," he said. "You might learn something."

● ● ●

With that sage advice ringing in my ears, I headed up to street level and hailed a cab. In those days, New York taxis came in every color that DuPont could think up. This one was a genuine Checker, bright blue with yellow trim. I told the driver to take me to Madison and 57th. He was a studious-looking kid, with a green sun visor, who was listening to the news on Pacifica Radio. An excited young woman with a French accent was being interviewed about the student riots that had been raging in Paris for several days.

"We could use something like that here," said the kid.

"You haven't had enough of that stuff for a while?" I asked.

"Just the beginning," said the kid. "The blacks aren't the only ones who are disenfranchised."

Under other circumstances, I'd have talked to him some more, but after what had just happened on the subway platform, I couldn't handle small talk. I was dying for a spliff, and I suspect the driver would have been cool with that, so long as I shared, but I couldn't afford to be more spooked than I already was. I just settled back and listened to the radio. "Cars overturned... Cobblestones pried loose and thrown at the police...President de Gaulle to make a speech on radio and television..."

"Another lame-dog president in the making," said the cabbie, "just like Johnson."

The Gruen Gallery was in the Fuller Building, an imposing deco slab on the northeast corner of Madison and 57th. To get to the gallery, you crossed a lobby with inlaid marble floors that exuded corporate wealth, then rose in an elevator entered by way of elaborate bronze-paneled doors celebrating the heroic accomplishments of the construction industry. Gruen's walls were currently devoted to a show by some third-rate stain painter who didn't merit a second look. Gruen was not there.

"He's on a studio visit," I was told.

My informant was Lena, Gruen's receptionist, who I had nearly slept with once after a chance encounter at The No Name Bar. I don't remember what went wrong, but whatever it was she didn't hold it against me. It may have been a bit of luck that she was there alone, because Lena liked to talk, and not having an inhibiting boss around loosened her tongue. I let her gossip for a while—about the imminent divorce of one of the gallery's artists and the financial scandal brewing around an ambitious young dealer who had just opened a large new space a dozen blocks uptown—then I sprang a casual question about Jerry Pedrosian.

"Does he sell much, these days?"

"Not as much as he did," said Lena, "but he has one or two steady collectors."

"Women?"

Lena giggled.

"You know Jerry," she said. "Norbert would kill me if he heard me saying this, but to be honest, Jerry's work hasn't been moving, and he's pretty bitter about it."

"I know of someone who might be interested in his stuff," I said, "but I guess Jerry's out of town."

"You can give me their name," she said. "I'll pass it on to Norbert."

"Where does Jerry go?" I threw out, hoping for the best.

"That's the thing," said Lena. "Nobody knows, but he's been taking these trips every few weeks. At least, that's what he tells us, and anyway he's certainly out of circulation. He usually disappears for about a week at a time. Doesn't leave a number. No one knows how to reach him, and we've no idea why he's being so mysterious. Just last month, Norbert had a nice sale lined up, but he couldn't find Jerry, so the client went down the hall and bought a Morris Louis instead."

I managed a couple more minutes of small talk, and flirted a little, so as not to seem too hung up on Pedrosian, before telling Lena I'd see her around. One thought that had popped into my head while I was chatting her up was that another tenant of the Fuller Building was Mark Kalindi. Mark was a dealer in nineteenth-century prints, drawings, and watercolors. I'd known him since my days with the DA's office when he had drawn my attention to some fake Turners that an Englishman decked out in a Savile Row suit and an Old Etonian tie was attempting to peddle. The Old Etonian tie might have worked in London, but it didn't help much in New York, and we eventually tracked down the perpetrator, a British actor who had failed to make his mark on, off, or off-off-Broadway. I had stayed in touch with Mark, and I remembered now that he has a daughter at Teddington, which made him worth a visit.

Mark was a large man, with a rather florid complexion, whose suit was permanently rumpled. His haystack of blond hair was always on the point of insubordination. He was, in fact, the last person you would expect to be a connoisseur of the delicate arts that were his specialty. He greeted me warmly, and, knowing that I am partial to the quiet subtleties of watercolor, showed me a pair of Winslow Homer drawings he had recently acquired at auction. When the moment was ripe, I asked him how Gemma was doing at Teddington.

"She loves it," he said, with an enthusiastic smile. "The right place for her, I think."

"I forget who," I said, "but someone who has a kid there was saying that he found the place too liberal, too unstructured."

"What's wrong with liberal?" he asked. "I suppose a place like Teddington could be unnerving for someone who lacks a good sense of who she is, but that's not Gemma's problem."

"Whoever this was said something about having a hard time with people like Jerry Pedrosian giving workshops."

Mark grinned.

"Gemma was at one of Pedrosian's seminars. The topic was art as protest and protest as art. She loved it. Knowing Jerry, it was probably bullshit, but that's the kind of stuff kids should be thinking about at that age. I don't know who your friend is, but you can tell him that from me, if you like."

I thanked him.

"I presume," he said, "that you're on a case?"

SIX

I stopped by the office to check my messages. There were a couple from J & V Air-Kool and one from Janice.

"Are you cradle-snatching now? I stayed at your place and made breakfast, and a dishy little blonde rang the doorbell. Not so little, actually, but very young and definitely dishy. She was surprised to see me—seemed nervous, almost frightened—and asked if you were home. When I said no she took off. Wouldn't leave a message."

Lydia? It looked like I was making a habit of being at the wrong place at the wrong time. If she—or whoever it was—knew where I lived and where I had my office, surely she must also know my phone number? Nothing tricky about the way I was listed.

I gave Andrea Marshall's number a try. No reply, which didn't surprise me, but still annoyed me. I wanted to hear her voice. Then I called downstairs for a sandwich, and while I was eating it, I heard the elevator arrive at my floor, and its door close as someone either left or entered. There were people up and down the corridor all day long, and if you had sat at my desk for as long as I had, you got a sense of where they were headed—Monica the psychotherapist in 3D, maybe, Dr. Joe the orthodontist in 3F, Olga the Swedish masseuse in 3G. I didn't hear anything that fit any familiar scenario so, because everything that was going on was spooking me, I went to the door and opened it.

"Freeze!" someone screamed in my ear.

A hulking uniformed cop was pressed against the wall to my right, his Colt Police Special pointed at my head, knees bent, body taut in the Weaver handgun stance you've seen in several hundred bad movies and TV shows.

I put my hands above my head.

"Don't fucking move!" he hissed.

Doors were being opened and people were peering out.

"Get back inside!" the cop yelled. The doors closed. Outside, sirens howled as police cruisers rushed to the scene, or maybe headed for a pizza pickup.

"Waiting for backup?" I asked, as politely as I could manage.

"Shut the fuck up!" he screamed.

I felt his spittle on my face. Cop spittle. He had a Joe Namath mustache. Mustaches were standard issue for the NYPD that year, and the Joe Namath was a popular model.

I heard the elevator ascend and open at my floor. The cop could not see who emerged from it because it was behind his back.

"Okay, you," the cop yelled, "stay in that fucking elevator, press a button—any button—and get the fuck outta here."

The man who had stepped from the elevator was a stubby individual in a seersucker jacket that looked a size too small. He had a faded blond crew cut and a rosy, clean-shaven face. It was okay for plainclothes officers to be clean-shaven. I was glad to see this one, Detective First Grade Campbell. I had had dealings with Campbell when I was with the DA's office. We talked the same language, more or less.

"You can put it down, Pelacci," he said.

The uniformed cop seemed to recognize the voice, which was low-pitched and raspy.

"There's a report of a man with a firearm," said the uniformed cop, keeping the revolver trained on my head. "I found this man here at the reported location."

"I heard that shit, too," said Campbell. "That's why I'm here. I'm enjoying a nice veggie burger and macrobiotic rice when I get a call for backup—and it seems there's not a uniformed officer in blocks thanks to this motherfucking slowdown. So I have to drag my sorry ass up here. There are umpteen thousand reports a day of someone with a firearm in New York City. I don't know what makes this one special, but the man whose brains you are threatening to blow out—while he may very well have a firearm in his possession—also has a license to carry one. Now put *yours* away, officer."

Slowly, the uniformed cop did as he was told. Campbell instructed me to show my investigator's license and my firearms license. I produced them and the uniformed cop scrutinized them, as if he was hoping to find something wrong. Campbell told him that he'd take care of things from there on, and indicated to me that we should step into my office. He sat down in the chair Mrs. Kravitz had occupied a few hours earlier, took out a pipe with a bowl carved in the shape of a devil's head, filled it with evil-looking black tobacco from a plastic pouch, then lit up with one of those special lighters that pipe smokers use.

"I smell chickadee," he said. "You've had a visitor?"

I ignored that.

"So what's this all about?" I asked.

"Like Officer Pelacci said," he told me, "there was a report of a person or persons with a gun in this building, in Suite 3B. That's where we're sitting now, I believe. Though whether I'd call it a suite…"

"Who called in this report?"

"Anonymous call to the emergency line. Any ideas?"

I shrugged.

"Could someone have seen that you were wearing a weapon—maybe spotted your holster under your jacket?"

"I'm not carrying a weapon. I don't often do the kind of work that calls for that kind of thing. I have a Smith & Wesson thirty-eight at my apartment, locked up in a closet."

I thought about the gun in the safe in my office, and felt for sure it was connected to the mysterious call, but I saw no way of bringing that into play without telling Campbell about a lot of things my employer would be unhappy to have the police know.

"So nobody," he said, "would have any reason to suppose there was someone armed in here?"

"I don't know when I last packed heat," I said.

"Strange," said Campbell, sucking on his pipe, which didn't seem to be functioning to his satisfaction.

"You've got me," I said.

"What are you working on these days?" he asked. "Anything that might tie in with this?"

"Bread-and-butter missing persons case. Teenage girl."

"A runaway?"

"That's what it looks like. She's probably getting stoned on Bourbon Street or in the Haight."

"Or streetwalking in Miami," said Campbell, getting to his feet. He nodded good-bye and turned toward the door, then paused.

"Nothing you should be telling me?" he said. "Nothing slipped your mind?"

"Nothing," I assured him.

● ● ●

Like many NYPD detective-investigators, Campbell had started in narcotics, then put in a spell in vice, but had spent most of his career in a citywide command assigned to high-profile theft and fraud, usually working undercover. Whether or not that was his current beat, I had no idea, but I knew he had a nose for anything bent, and I was pretty sure he hadn't bought into me playing dumb. I had no idea whether he would be interested in what I might be hiding, but the fact that we had had this little encounter just added to the gumbo. I had been on this investigation for less than twenty-four hours, and I was beginning to feel that it was running me rather than the other way around.

I had to do something, and the only thing I could think of that made sense was to get back to tracking down Pedrosian. Somebody must know where he was. I called the gallery to see if Norbert Gruen was back from his studio visit. He was, but he didn't add much to what I already knew.

"He just takes off once in a while. He's a big boy. I'm his dealer, not his nursemaid. Anyway, why would I tell you? I know what line of business you're in. For all I know, you want to nail him for something."

My phone had a long cord, and as I spoke to Gruen, I walked over to the window to see if the rain had arrived. The clouds were low and threatening, but the street below seemed to be dry. Then I saw her—a girl with long blond hair in jeans and a light-colored raincoat, standing on the far side of the road at the edge of the park, looking up at my window. She seemed to sense that I had spotted her, turned, and began to walk away, quickly, toward the George Washington statue. I hurried out of my office, ran down the stairs, and rushed out into the street—where Detective Campbell was standing, minding his own business, or maybe mine.

He removed his pipe from his mouth and twisted up his face.

"It's not pulling today," he confided. "Happens with weather like this."

● ● ●

Ten minutes later, oversize raindrops were spattering down on the sidewalks, and then the skies unloaded. I had been searching, without much hope, for the girl I had seen from my window, who might have been Lydia Kravitz though I didn't get a good enough look at her to be sure. Girls were ironing their hair as a fashion statement, so it was no surprise that I spotted several girls with straight blond hair, but none of them fit the profile. When the rain came down, I took shelter in the doorway of S. Klein and just waited there. After all, if she was looking for me—Lydia or whoever—it was probably a sensible idea just to stay put and let her find me. I must have stood there for half an hour but nothing happened, except that I held the door open for a lot of nice bargain-hunting ladies from the outer boroughs, loaded down with shopping bags and looking pretty damned pleased with themselves.

I did have a thought, though. Those ladies made me think about parents. Unless they were dead, Jerry Pedrosian must have parents somewhere, and it occurred to me that I knew someone nearby who might have a bead on them. When the rain let up a bit, I bought a folding umbrella from a guy on the street and headed downtown on 4th Avenue, which in those days was still home to half a dozen secondhand bookstores. My destination was Marquis Rare Books and Manuscripts, a store that was not quite as high-toned as the name implied, though it was a good place to browse if you had a couple of hours to kill.

Used bookstores smell great in the rain. The books seem to come alive—more alive, in fact, than the elderly assistant who sat behind the desk with a Mickey Spillane paperback in front of him. I think I woke him and he resented it.

I asked for Steve, the owner, and the assistant jerked his thumb toward the rear of the building. I found Steve Schuller in the back room, sorting through cartons of books, putting them into different piles. I knew Steve because I often came to him when I was looking for out-of-print art books that I needed for research. What I had remembered was that Steve had grown up in the same Bronx neighborhood as Pedrosian. They didn't much like each other, but their parents had been friends who played gin rummy and pinochle together. I told Steve that I was looking for Pedrosian in connection with a case.

"You gonna send him away for a while?" he asked hopefully.

"I'm looking for him for information about somebody else," I said, trying to be as vague as possible. "He's out of town and I haven't been able to track him down. Are his parents still alive?"

"His father passed away, but his mother's still hanging on— just. She's down in Florida, near my folks—Lauderdale Lakes, a place called Hawaiian Gardens. My mother still sees her—bakes her cookies—but she says Millie's mind is slipping."

That was a blow.

"I tell you what, though," said Steve. "Jerry's got an aunt Ida who's still up in the Bronx, on West Tremont. Refuses to leave. They were all in that same building once, and since Jerry's mother had a part-time job—his father was always sickly, something with the lungs—Jerry and his sister spent as much time with Aunt Ida as in their own apartment."

I asked if he knew how to reach her.

"I think she's still in the same place, but my mom will know for sure,"

He picked up the phone and soon had the phone number and address.

"Keep your eye on your wallet while you're up there. And anything else you hold dear. I was up in the old neighborhood recently, and it's scary. The whole area is run by gangs—Black Spades, Ghetto Brothers, Savage Nomads. Fort Apache is just down the street."

"What about Jerry's sister?" I asked.

"Shirley? I heard she married some kind of public figure. Can't think who. She was something though—the local sweater girl. We thought she was Lana Turner incarnate."

I used Steve's phone to call Aunt Ida. She swore at me and told me to leave her alone. That was before I had said a word. I told her I was a friend of her nephew Jerry. She said that was my problem, not hers. I asked if she knew how I could get hold of Jerry. She asked how much he owed me, adding that she had no intention of helping him out. I told her it wasn't about money.

"So is it your wife or your daughter?" she asked.

Then she cackled with laughter and coughed—a hacking, three-pack-a-day-cough—told me to go to hell, and hung up on me.

"Nice lady," I said to Steve. "Old school."

"I should have warned you," he said. "She always was kind of cantankerous. We used to call her and her hubby the commies, because they were always ranting about how America has betrayed the People. Ranting is her style."

"At least I know she's at home," I said.

"In that neighborhood," he replied, "she probably never leaves the house."

● ● ●

I didn't really feel like schlepping up to the Bronx, so I tried Andrea Marshall's number again. Still no reply, which was still annoying. I wanted to talk to her again. There seemed to be no good alternative to paying Aunt Ida a call, but I decided to forego the pleasures of a subway ride to the Bronx, followed by a hike through tribal territory, and instead walked over to University Place where there was a parking garage that rented used cars as a sideline. I negotiated with Frankie, who I'd dealt with many times, and got a good rate on a Datsun with a bushel of miles on the clock, faded paintwork, and a jagged dent in the left rear fender. It was the kind of vehicle that would fit right in where I was going.

The rain was over for the time being, and as I headed north, sunlight was flashing off the Hudson River, where a cruise liner was setting out for somewhere romantic with palm trees and daiquiris. My destination was free of such distractions. Even before I left Manhattan, I passed plenty of burned-out buildings. In the Bronx, whole blocks had been torched and entire neighborhoods were deserted, except for the street corners that were home to clusters of junkies selling or nodding off. I made it to West Tremont without incident, and found a parking place between a battered Firebird and a rust-pitted Imperial. I was wrong about the Datsun fitting in. In this company, it passed for near mint condition.

Aunt Ida's building had once had pretensions of class. A flight of curving steps led to an entrance topped with an ogee arch. The roofline was interrupted by a decorative turret equipped with vertical slots like the ones archers fired arrows through when a castle was under siege. I couldn't help thinking they might come in handy. The windows of at least one apartment were boarded up, the steps were littered with broken glass and discarded needles, and the walls were disfigured by early modern graffiti tags, Taki 183 vintage. I picked my way up the steps and entered the unlit lobby, which smelled of piss and vomit. A group of hoods was hanging there, some sitting on the stairs, some lounging around in their Converse Chuckie Ts, passing a can of Bud, and waiting for someone in Osaka to invent the boom box. They sized me up from under their baseball caps with expressions that rated minus on the Emily Post gracious welcome scale. I figured they had me pegged as the Man, and I didn't aim to disabuse them of the idea, though in that neighborhood, cops usually traveled in pairs.

"I'm looking for an old woman—Mrs. Pedrosian," I said.

Everybody looked to a kid in a T-shirt that had "Friendly Freddie" printed across the chest. He was skinny as a thin dime, but in this crowd, he was Mister Phat. He looked through me for awhile, then said, "Bitch gotta mouth on her."

I wasn't sure if he was referring to Mrs. Pedrosian or to me.

"5C," said Friendly Freddie, looking through me some more.

There was an elevator, but no one in his right mind would have taken it, so I walked up the stairs, past piles of garbage, past the smell of something greasy being cremated on a hotplate, past a man kissing the shoulder of a girl who was half hanging out of a torn nightdress, past an old dude in rags asleep on a cot on a landing, till I came to 5C. I rapped on the door. Nothing happened for a couple of minutes. I knocked again, and a voice I recognized from the phone yelled, "Hold your horses!"

I yelled, "Police!"

There's a law against impersonating a police officer, but it only applies where the term "law abiding" has some kind of currency.

Through the door, I could hear the *tap tap* of someone walking with a cane—very slowly.

"How do I know you're cops? I didn't call the cops."

"Ma'am—I'm a police officer who needs to ask a few questions. Nothing to be afraid of."

"Why would I be afraid of the cops? And don't call me ma'am. A ma'am is a cheap broad who runs a whorehouse."

She had, at last, begun to unfasten locks—a lot of them.

"Why is it," she said, "that when I call the police, nobody comes? But when I don't call…"

The door opened about six inches, but the chain was still on. Fierce gray eyes stared up at me through bottle-glass lenses. Aunt Ida was about two hands taller than a mule, and looked twice as ornery. She removed an un-tipped cigarette from between parched lips.

"At least you're better looking than the last ones they sent," she said, "and you look like you could probably chase down a purse-snatcher without having a coronary. That's our taxes they're padding their guts with. Who told them to do that?"

I admitted I had no idea.

"Now," she said, "what do you want?"

She made no move to release the chain that held the door.

"Could I come in, please?" I asked.

"I can answer questions from here," she said, "without a bull-horn. I know my rights, young man. I'm not some wet-behind-the-ears pushover. You got questions—unless you've got a war-rant you spit 'em out from where you are."

"I just thought it would be more comfortable—"

"Comfortable? For who? For you? I suppose you're worried about those kids downstairs? Yeah—they're scary, but how did they get that way? Because America gave them the shaft, that's how. I'm watching the television the other day, and some fat fuck from City Hall says kids like that would be okay if they didn't play hooky from school. What do they learn in school? Someone tells them that everyone's born equal. Bullshit! After you've been fed that kind of crap and you come home to this kind of shit, you're not gonna believe anything they feed you. They tell you one and one is two, and you want to know, 'Says who? Why should I believe that? Feels like three to me.'"

I gave up on trying to talk my way into the apartment.

"I just wanted to ask a couple of questions about your nephew Jerry."

"Was it you that called earlier? Okay, you heard what I said then—that's all I've got to say."

"Mrs. Pedrosian—if you've got any idea where I could reach him—"

"First of all, why would I tell you? What's he accused of?"

"He isn't accused of anything. It's not like that. We think he could help us with an investigation."

"Yeah—I bet that's what they said to Sacco and Vanzetti, and look what happened to them."

"We're not talking Sacco and Vanzetti," I said.

"You talk about who you want to talk about," said Aunt Ida. "I'll talk about Sacco and Vanzetti. I went up to Boston, to the courthouse, to protest. I was there. Let's talk about Emma Goldman. Let's talk about the Rosenbergs. Railroaded, all of 'em."

"This is not that kind of case," I said. "Jerry might be able to help us with a missing persons investigation."

"I might have known there'd be a woman involved," said Aunt Ida.

"As a matter of fact, it does involve a woman."

"Jesus Christ—of course it involves a woman. We're talking about Jerry. So, big deal. Anyway, what makes you think I would know where he is? Jerry's the big-time artist now. Hangs out with Nelson Rockefeller and a bunch of filthy plutocrats. He calls once in a while—came to see me once on my birthday—offered to buy me a plane ticket down to Florida. Why would I want to go to Florida? Play canasta with a bunch of old farts who've sold their souls for a condo with a view of a swamp? Stand meekly on line in a cafeteria for the blue-plate special? Florida! It's full of Republicans. I raised money for the Abraham Lincoln Brigade, for Christ's sake!"

"About Jerry…"

"What about him? He's not a bad boy. I tried to teach him right, because he didn't get much—what should I call it?—ethical guidance from his parents. All they wanted was a Buick and a picket fence on Long Island. Yeah, I have an address and telephone number for Jerry, but I'm sure you've got those, too."

"What about his sister?"

"Shirley? Don't tell me you want to speak to that bitch?"

"I thought she might have some idea where Jerry is."

Aunt Ida laughed.

"You don't know Jerry, and you certainly don't know Shirley. They don't have much to do with each other. I haven't spoken to her since I found out she was campaigning for Barry Goldwater. Then I heard she married that Neanderthal windbag Don Baldridge. That was the end. She belongs in the salt mines."

Donald Baldridge was a Republican councilman known for his far-reaching ambitions and reactionary views.

"And now," said Aunt Ida, "if you'll excuse me, young man, it's time for me to watch *Jeopardy!*"

She slammed the door in my face. Too bad. I would have enjoyed talking to Aunt Ida some more.

I walked down the stairs—past the sleeping bum, past the necking couple, past the smell of burning fat, past the garbage, and past the gangstas in the lobby. As I descended the front steps to the street, somebody behind me yelled "muthafucka," but I let it go. I half-expected to find the Datsun trashed, but it seemed to be untouched, so I unlocked it, got in, and started the motor. The car did not explode. I eased out of the parking space, and just as I was about to pull into traffic, I heard a loud crack, and a bullet smacked into the safety glass a foot from my left ear, passed through the driver's side headrest, and lodged in the framework of the right side rear door. I hit the gas and didn't slow down till I reached the Cross Bronx Expressway.

Probably just a fond farewell from Friendly Freddie and his boys, but the way things had been going I couldn't discount any possibility.

SEVEN

I drove back to Manhattan, and stopped for a bite at a coffee shop on 96th Street. In the phone book, I discovered that Donald and Shirley Baldridge were listed at a Park Avenue address that figured to be somewhere in the 70s. I called their number, and the phone was answered by a woman with a West Indian accent. She told me Mrs. Baldridge was not at home. I asked if she knew when Mrs. Baldridge would be back. She said that Mrs. Baldridge was at a reception, and she had no idea how long it would last. Someone had left a late edition of the *News* in the phone booth. I took it back to my booth and combed it for stories on Republican receptions or rallies. It didn't take me long to discover that there was a fundraising event for Richard Nixon at the St. Regis Hotel that evening.

It was already getting dark outside, so I headed for the St. Regis, passing the Baldridges' apartment on my way. Nothing could have provided a greater contrast to Aunt Ida's building than this grandiose pile, lit up like a drunken stiff in a screwball comedy, with not one, but two costumed doormen swaggering on the sidewalk, fly casting for taxis to stuff mink-wrapped matrons into. I continued south to 55th Street and left the Datsun at a ten-bucks-an-hour underground parking garage, earning looks of pity and derision.

I had been to the St. Regis a couple of times when I was working on a case that involved truckloads of fake Salvador Dali prints. Dali maintained a suite there for himself, his old lady Gala, and his pet ocelots. It's where he once told Ali MacGraw to take her clothes off, and then sucked her toes. Dali didn't suck my toes, or even ask me to undress, but it was a trip anyway.

I doubt if Richard Nixon ever sucked anybody's toes, but the thought of him peeling off Pat's pantyhose and having a go is humbling. In any case, he was running for president—again—and serial home owners with Gestapo haircuts were prepared to pay four figures to be in the same room as him, even though they could have watched him make a fool of himself for free on *Laugh-In*. That night, he was in town after winning a primary in some sparsely populated territory west of the Hudson. He was addressing the faithful from the stage of the St. Regis Roof Ballroom, and the media was out in force to cover the event, with television vans parked along 55th and photographers clutching their Speed Graphics at the entrance. That made it easy for me. I had the slovenly, down-at-the-heel, seen-it-all, this-guy-must-work-for-the-tabloids look down pat, and it didn't hurt that a couple of the photographers knew me and greeted me by name as I strolled into the hotel. I didn't even need to use my fake press pass. The doorman and porters ignored me, and the two spooks in dark glasses—dressed in Johnny Carson suits with three-button jackets tailored to conceal their weapons—barely looked me over. Even after Dallas, and after Martin had been shot in Atlanta, security was still pretty lax at these affairs. Who would want to harm a white guy with a five-o'clock shadow just because he wanted to hang his hat in the White House? That changed forever a couple of weeks later, when Bobby went down for the count.

I rode up in an elevator and stepped out into the lobby adjacent to the ballroom. Staff and media people were milling around, trying not to trip over the cables that snaked into the ballroom. As a door opened, I caught a glimpse of the future president addressing the GOP groupies.

"My opponents are three peas in a pod," he chortled, attempting to sound folksy. "There's not a shred of difference between them."

That produced a smattering of applause and a polite undertow of what passes for laughter in Republican neighborhoods.

It was about then that I spotted Donald Baldridge, who I recognized from his frequent appearances on local news shows. He had slicked-back hair and wore a tuxedo with a red cummerbund, which did nothing to distract attention from an expanding waistline. He was standing near one of the doors to the ballroom, arguing in whispers with a woman in a low-cut black dress and a black lace bolero jacket. Going only on Steve Schuller's description of her as a former neighborhood sweater girl, I was prepared to bet that this was Mrs. Baldridge. It must have been twenty-something years since her Lana Turner phase, but she was still a striking woman with a figure that begged for attention. Her face, however, was distorted with rage, and she seemed on the verge of tears. Donald Baldridge hissed something that caused the woman to freeze, as if she had been smacked across the face, then he pivoted on his heel, and returned to the ballroom.

Mrs. Baldridge didn't try to hold back the tears anymore. They poured down her cheeks, and she didn't even attempt to wipe them away. I moved in closer, just as she headed for the elevator. I joined her and couldn't help noticing that she smelled very nice. She was too preoccupied to pay any attention to me—not sobbing, just weeping silently, with an occasional heave of the shoulders. When she exited, she headed for the King Cole Bar, and I followed at a discreet distance. The room was full of tourists drinking Red Snappers because that's what the guide books say you're supposed to drink at the King Cole Bar. Mel Tormé, or one of those smooth guys, had just finished a set and there was the babble of chatter that comes after five choruses of *Mountain Greenery*. Mrs. Baldridge was approached by a waiter, who offered her a table, but she shook her head and walked to the bar where she grabbed a perch. There was an empty bar stool next to her so I moseyed over and asked if she was expecting anyone. She shook her head, without looking at me. The barman placed a martini in front of her, and asked me what I was having. I ordered a Dewar's and soda, no ice. Mrs. Baldridge sipped her cocktail, ate the olive, played with the swizzle stick, and stared at the Maxfield Parrish mural behind the bar, tears still trickling down her cheeks, a few dripping onto her impressive cleavage.

I took my time, then said, "Excuse me—are you okay, lady?"

She looked at me, sardonically and said, "Do I look okay, sonny?"

"You seem upset."

"I've got to hand it to you," she said. "Your powers of observation are remarkable. You should be a detective or something."

"I always loved Dick Tracy in the Sunday funnies," I said, "and Rip Kirby, too."

"Yeah? Brenda Starr was more my cup of tea. I always thought I'd grow up to be a girl reporter. That seemed pretty glamorous."

"I know what you mean—Brenda Starr, Hildy Johnson."

"Yeah, Hildy was bitchin'."

She stared at me, swallowed the rest of her martini at a single gulp, and asked what I was drinking. I told her I was okay, but she insisted on buying me another scotch.

"I know who you are," she said, showing the first signs of the booze having hit. "You're one of those boy reporters. You're here to cover Tricky Dick."

I didn't say I wasn't.

"Drink up," she said. "You don't look like Cary Grant, but you'll do."

I wasn't sure what she meant by that, but I obliged.

"I might have a story for you," she said. "Do you know who I am?"

"You're the very attractive wife of Councilman Baldridge," I said.

She liked that.

"Maybe you are Cary Grant," she said.

"I can do the accent, too," I told her.

"Don't spoil it. So, I guess it wasn't an accident that you sat down next to me?"

"Yes and no. You probably didn't notice, but I was in the elevator when you came down from the ballroom. I knew who you were because I'd seen you with Councilman Baldridge earlier. I couldn't miss that you were upset, so I followed you to the bar because that's what sneaky people like me do. The stool next to you was open..."

She had already drunk most of her second martini, and now she smiled a puckered smile, placing a hand on my knee.

"So," she said, "are you in pursuit of a story, or is it the councilman's wife that you're interested in?"

"You never know where you're going to find a good story," I said.

With her fingers spread, she touched a snowy expanse of bosom, batted her eyelids in my general direction, and took another gulp of her martini.

"You don't know how true that is," she said.

I figured I'd better put out a feeler before the booze really hit.

"If I remember right," I said, "you have a brother who's a well-known artist."

Her expression changed.

"You were doing so well," she said, "and now you have to go and bring him up."

"Sorry," I said. "I didn't realize that was a touchy subject."

"If Jerry's involved," she said, "it's a touchy subject."

"I brought up his name only because I used to drink with Jerry, once in a while," I improvised. "He used to come into a bar called The Red Lion, down in the Village. It's a hangout for journalists, but it gets artists, too."

"Jerry never did care who he drank with," said Shirley the sweater girl, "so long as there were cute waitresses around, and someone to pick a fight with."

"Yeah, he got into a few fights," I said, hoping to unlock some more sisterly insights.

"Usually," she said, "they start with art or politics. He thinks he knows more about both than anyone else. I know fuck-all about art, but he knows shit about politics. He's a half-baked lefty through and through. Got it from our aunt Ida."

She signaled to the barman to bring her another drink.

I asked if she was sure she needed one.

"Don't *you* start getting on my ass," she said. "You're not even a councilman. Do you realize that my regular fuck is going to be the next goddam mayor? If I don't kill him first."

"The future mayor didn't seem to be treating you very nicely upstairs."

"Nicely? What's that supposed to mean? Were you spying on us or something?"

"I couldn't help seeing you were fighting."

"Lucky for him, it was in a public place; otherwise, I'd have castrated him with my nail scissors."

"It's none of my business, but..."

"Fucking A it's none of your business," she said. She hesitated for a tipsy moment then continued, "But if you're a newsman, maybe I could make it your business. You want a scoop, sonny? You stick with me, and maybe I'll tell you something that will curl your hair—and straighten out other parts of your anatomy."

This kind of dialogue continued for a while longer, until she finished her third martini. Then she waited till I caught up with her, though she took the last two fingers of my scotch for herself. Afterward, she tottered from the bar stool and with studied nonchalance adjusted her shoulder straps for the benefit of interested onlookers.

"Let's get out of here before the warbler gets back," she said. "I know that bird. He'll just sing something sad and get me weepy again."

At the hotel entrance, she told a doorman to call one of the hacks—the horse-drawn carriages catering to tourists—from the rank on 59th Street. Ten minutes later, during which time Mrs. Baldridge struck some choice poses for bored paparazzi, a trim-looking buggy, drawn by a pony with ribbons in its mane, and driven by a tough-looking broad in Annie Oakley drag, clattered to a halt. We clambered aboard, and in another ten minutes, we had swished into Central Park, and were trotting along somewhere near the Wollman Rink.

I don't know why, but hacks were somehow immune to the mayhem that was otherwise endemic to Central Park after dark. Maybe they paid protection. Maybe there were little people—the Leprechauns of the Sheep's Meadow—riding shotgun. In any case, the sky was mostly clear that evening, and there was a sliver of waning moon, which was outshone by the trellises of light bordering the park. It was mild for that time of the year, but Mrs. Baldridge snuggled up to me as though she were freezing. I noticed again that she smelled nice—Lancôme something or other, blended with a generous whiff of Smirnoff and musky effusions from beneath Mrs. Baldridge's clothing—but I warned myself that volatile emanations alone were not grounds for unprofessional behavior. There was also her cleavage, now available for closer inspection, which aroused fantasies of spelunking in fleshy caverns. Nothing wrong, I concluded, in putting a protective arm around her. She snuggled closer.

If this sounds romantic, it wasn't. It was weird and faintly disturbing, but undeniably sexy. Shirley Baldridge was a woman who was incapable of not agitating the surface of any nearby reservoir of testosterone, and stimulating the adjacent glands, as I could now bear witness. The surreally erotic setting, and the rhythmic motion of the hack as it bounced along, did not help my efforts to resist her allure. At the same time, common sense, and a vestigial sense of old school manners, told me to keep my pants zippered.

Shirley's politics are anathema to everything you believe in, I told myself.

But then again, didn't James Bond make out with Tatiana Romanova? And did Bond lose sleep over the geopolitical implications of that? On top of which, my political antennae had been dulled by the fact that I had drunk three scotches, which Mrs. Baldridge had, after all, graciously paid for. And the King Cole's barman was famous for pouring generous measures.

At those prices, he had to be.

I felt a little bit like Brer Rabbit stuck to the Tar Baby, but there was no Brer Fox around, so I had only myself to plead with.

Whatever you do, I silently begged, *don't throw me into that briar patch.*

"You're awful quiet for a reporter," said Mrs. Baldridge. "I didn't think they came in a thoughtful model, except when it comes to dreaming up un-American lies for the editorial pages. How long have you been in the racket?"

"A long time."

"It can't be that long. How old are you, honey?"

She didn't wait for me to answer.

"I'd figure about eight or ten years younger than me," she said. I didn't argue.

"Okay, so it's imperative for me to ask, do you find me attractive?"

"Of course I do."

The situation wasn't getting any easier.

"For an older woman?"

"You're a very attractive woman—period."

Sexy would have been a better way of putting it, but I could live with attractive.

"Fuckable?" she said. "I mean, let's not beat around the briar patch."

Now the woman was reading my mind. I struggled to free myself from the clutches of the metaphorical tar baby and hang on to my objectivity, but couldn't find a way.

"I would have to say so," I admitted.

"You'd think my husband would notice that," said Mrs. Baldridge, "wouldn't you?"

"He's blind if he doesn't."

"He doesn't even look at me anymore," said Mrs. Baldridge. "Okay, he looks at me, but he doesn't see me. I get undressed and I put on a nice negligee, and he doesn't see that I've hoisted my signals."

She burst into tears again—sobbing this time—grabbed my right hand in both of hers, and crushed it to her bosom.

"Easy, girl," said the driver to her pony.

It took Mrs. Baldridge quite a while to pull herself together, during which time her chest heaved fetchingly, and she moved one hand to my thigh.

"Listen," she said, "here's the deal. You know that trashy weather girl on Kip Lester's newscast? The one with the cat eyes and the big boobs—though they're kind of droopy, aren't they?—and the lisp that's supposed to be sexy?"

"Breeze Daniels?"

"Bweeze Daniels, my ass. Bwidget Danichevski from Astowia. They call her Bweeze because it's a bweeze to get into her pants. When she bothers to wear any."

It didn't take much detective work to figure what was coming next.

"Don has been screwing the little cunt. He met her when he was at the studio to do an interview with Kip. The bitch had on one of those teeny-weeny miniskirts that she wears, and she flashed her pussy at him, like it's saying, 'Here I am, come and pet me...' He actually came home and told me about it—pretended to laugh the whole thing off. 'I just thought I'd share this amusing anecdote with you, darling. Can you imagine this little whore thinking I'd fall for such a crude attempt at seduction? What does she take me for? A Kennedy Democrat?' What he forgot to mention was that he'd already fed his teeny wiener to her sweet little pussy. To make things that much choicer, they had been getting it off in a rental apartment in a house belonging to me—down by Gramercy Park—which happened to be empty except, conveniently, for a queen-size bed. How do you like those latkes? I found out about this fooling around a couple of months ago, and he swore it was over. Then today, I discovered he was still fucking her. That's your story, pal. Take it to your editor, and tell him to do what he likes with it. But first, you owe me."

There was no ambiguity about what she meant. She hitched up her dress, and I saw that she was wearing not the ubiquitous baggy panty hose of that bygone era, but old-fashioned stockings, held up by garters, worn fetchingly with slinky black lingerie. When she dressed that evening, she had not been thinking of hurrying home to watch reruns of *The Honeymooners.*

"You can see I was going to be generous to someone tonight, sweetheart. I owe that much to myself. You turned out to be the lucky party."

She took my hand again, and placed it on her crotch. They fit together nicely, and I was glad I had clean nails, but a decision had to be made. My libido pointed out, quite forcibly, that I hadn't fucked anybody but my ex-wife in close to three months, while at the same time, my conscience warned me that my honorary membership in the Philip Marlowe Hardboiled but Strictly Ethical Order of Investigative Chivalry was on the line. I was like some Looney Tunes character with a devil perched on one shoulder and an angel on the other, fighting it out. The devil was armed with a pitchfork, while the angel had only a halo to defend her honor.

Reluctantly, I removed my hand from Mrs. Baldridge's underwear.

"You better hear me out," I told her. "Here's the bottom line. I'm not a reporter. There's not going to be any story in the papers tomorrow. I'm here under false pretenses."

Mrs. Baldridge stared at me for a long moment or two then slapped me hard across the face."

"Good girl," said the driver, urging her pony to a canter.

"If you could drop me at Columbus Circle," I said, "that would be convenient."

Mrs. Baldridge seethed for a few seconds, then grabbed my hand and bit it hard before replacing it on her lingerie, which had a therapeutic effect.

"I didn't come this far to be ditched," she said. "You owe me, and maybe I owe you because you've saved me from making a total fool of myself. My God, you could have been a real reporter, then nothing would've spared me from a humiliating future as the pathetic bitch whose ex married that trashy weather girl—the one who's now first lady of New York City. I'd have to move to New Rochelle to escape the shame."

She closed her eyes and sighed, as if the specter of exile in Westchester County was overwhelming.

"What are we waiting for?" she asked, biting my ear this time.

I bit her back, but not on the ear.

"That's more like it," said Mrs. Baldridge. "Take your time," she called out to the girl driving the carriage, "and we'll take ours."

EIGHT

When we got back to the hotel, Donald Baldridge was standing outside with a gaggle of politicos and their wives lined up for taxis and limos. Mrs. Baldridge waited till she was sure that he had spotted us, then gave me a long, rather sloppy kiss, and straightened my tie before she stepped down to the sidewalk, where she paused to studiously tug at her skirt before walking up to her husband and giving him a peck on the cheek. Only then did she turn toward me and call out, for the benefit of the assembled Republican dignitaries, "Call me soon, babe. I'll be waiting."

The carriage driver, who had been well paid and entertained, took me to the garage where I had left the rented car. I drove to my apartment, and found a parking space half a block away. My luck was turning. I half-expected to find the mysterious blond girl waiting for me, but there was no one around except Eartha, a six-foot-four drag queen who had once had a tryout with the Knicks, and was now an unrestricted free agent plying her wares along the waterfront. She was propped up on my stoop, smoking.

"My arse is sore," she said, affecting a British accent, "these 'eels are killing me, and this is my last faggy."

I gave her half a pack of Gauloises and went inside. I took a shower, which made me feel a bit better, and rolled a joint. I had been avoiding dope since the IRT incident, but now I needed a hit. It had been just over twenty-four hours since I met with Kravitz. In that time I had been shot at, almost pushed into the path of a subway train, presented with a gun in a Bloomingdale's shopping bag, raided by the police, haunted by a blond girl who might or might not be Lydia Kravitz, made the acquaintance of Lydia's succulent mama, and fucked Jerry Pedrosian's sister while riding in Central Park. None of which got me any closer to knowing what the hell was going on.

And then there was Andrea, who had gotten under my skin despite a display of bad manners.

I fell asleep on the sofa and woke at a little after one. I doubted I was going to have much luck if I tried to go back to sleep, so I reheated the coffee Janice had brewed that morning, drank a cup, put on some jeans and a leather jacket, and walked down Hudson to a bar that had jazz till three in the morning. The combo that night was a piano-bass duo—bebop veterans who had played with Bird and the heavy dudes. I caught the last half of a set, and that invigorated me, so I went back to the car and drove to my office.

Walter was on duty again. I asked him if any more pretty blondes had been asking for me. No such luck, he told me. When I stepped out of the elevator on my floor, I was surprised to find a light on in the office of Olga the masseuse. She must have heard me, because she looked out.

"Mr. Detective," she said. "You've had a busy day."

She had on tight black leather pants, black patent boots with stiletto heels, and a low-cut black leather bustier that reminded me she had lovely shoulders.

"You're working pretty late yourself," I said.

"Like Mayor Lindsay keeps telling us," she said, "these are difficult times. I work when the client can get away from whoever or whatever he's getting away from."

A male voice inside her suite called out, "Are you coming back, for Chrissakes? I don't pay you to leave me dangling like this."

Olga shrugged.

"Remember," she said, "that offer of a free trial still stands."

Inside my office, I turned on the answering machine. A bill collector and an angry message from Gabriel Kravitz demanding to know what was going on. That was followed by a female voice so faint I had to play the message several times before I could understand any of what was being said, except for the first words, which were clear enough.

"Please help..."

The voice was young and frightened. Or maybe it was trying to sound frightened. After the request for help, the tape became unintelligible for several seconds, scrambled and distant. Then I could make out the words "maybe too late..." which emerged from an ocean of static. My guess was that the call was from a radio telephone. I had had some experience with these when I was undercover with the DA's office, and I knew that the service was highly unreliable in Manhattan because of the high-rise buildings. Whatever the case, there was another stretch of indecipherable interference before the words "top floor" followed by a fragment of what may have been an address. I could definitely make out the number—137—and was pretty sure the street name was Lazy Lane or Ladies Lane. Those didn't mean anything to me, so I checked them out in my *A to Z*. No Lazy Lane anywhere in the five boroughs, but I found a Ladies Lane in SoHo, a blip on the map that ran a single block from east to west, just north of Canal. I must have passed it dozens of times without noticing it.

When I got there, I saw why. It would be difficult for a street—just an alley really—to be more anonymous. It was badly lit, and barely wide enough for a single truck to pass through. The majority of structures in SoHo are six or seven stories tall, but here they were only three and four stories high. It was hard to make out much detail at 3:15 in the morning, but I could see that they were brick, rather than cast iron like the bulk of the district, and probably older than the typical SoHo property. Later, I learned that the street owed its name to the fact that in the middle of the nineteenth century, it was at the center of the red light district, though before that the buildings had been fashionable shops. Whatever architectural charm they may have had was compromised by the fact that they had been retrofitted at some point with clumsy fire escapes. Ladies Lane had been there when Charles Dickens made his first visit to New York in 1842, and it still possessed a distinctly Dickensian air.

I had parked the Datsun on Wooster, and I took a short stroll just to be sure everything was quiet. That part of town was kept free of garden-variety crime by the mob families who ran protection for the parents and *paisanos* who kept pigeons and hung out laundry in the neighborhood, but there was always the possibility of running into a couple of *soldatos* setting fire to a garbage truck owned by a rival family, or dropping off a body in the trunk of a stolen Eldorado with Jersey plates. That spring night, though, the area was as quiet as a morgue, and deserted except for rodents and the feral cats that darted from one bale of rags to the next.

The building at 137 Ladies Lane was much like the others on the alley, three bays wide, free of adornment. To the naked eye, it appeared empty—as abandoned as the houses in the Bronx I'd driven by a few hours earlier. I was in pretty good shape in those days, but the hinged ladder attached to the lowest platform of the fire escape was out of my reach unless I had something to climb on. I thought about driving the Datsun underneath the fire escape, and getting access by way of the vehicle's roof, but that was too risky. Blocking a narrow alley like that, the car was likely to attract attention. All it would take was some Barney in a passing patrol car to spot it, and I'd be in trouble. Then I noticed that there was a length of rope hanging down from the ladder. I hadn't spotted it at first because it was half-hidden and in a pool of darkness, but there it was, almost like an invitation. I couldn't quite reach it from ground level, but the loft district served as a communal garbage dump, and I was quickly able to locate a battered filing cabinet that provided the leg up I needed.

I pulled on the rope, and the ladder swung down noiselessly. I had expected some kind of rusty creak, but the fire escape appeared to be well maintained. I reached the first platform, hoping to get a glimpse into the building, but the windows were covered with old-fashioned roller blinds pulled fully down. That was par for the course around there because artists were often living illegally, and were careful to protect their turf from housing inspectors and other licensed predators. The blinds were pulled down on the next two floors, too, but on the fourth floor, the blinds on one window had been left open a few inches. I peered in, and gradually, my eyes adjusted to the faint light that was provided by the glow from a television set on the floor. It had been left on, and its screen danced with static. I could make out an open space with very little furniture. There was a big table with some objects on it that I could not decipher, a few kitchen chairs, the television set, and not much else that I could see. I was pretty sure that there was no one in that room, though that didn't mean there was nobody in some adjacent space, or on another floor. The fact that the television had been left on, though, was probably a good sign. At least, that's what I told myself.

I risked trying the windows, but they were all locked. Then I noticed that below one of them there was an opening provided for a room air conditioner. No air conditioner had been installed, and the opening was crudely blocked with plywood that I was able to remove without difficulty. I listened at the opening for a while. No noise inside. No snores or whispers, just the hiss of the TV. I took off my leather jacket, pushed it through the opening, then squeezed in after it. I used the baby flashlight I carry to take a quick look around. Not much that I hadn't spotted from outside, except for a couple of mattresses in one corner, a little table with an electric coffeemaker, and some shelves with a few books on them. It was the big table or, rather, what was sitting on it, that caught my attention. There was a radio telephone mounted in a briefcase, presumably the one that had been used to call me. An open carton, originally intended for some Heinz product, contained four .38-caliber Ruger semiautomatic pistols, just like the one in my office safe. Another one lay on the table, next to the carton. Also on the table, along with half-empty containers of Chinese food, was a submachine gun—an Uzi—plus a high-powered sporting rifle fitted with a telescopic sight, and clips of ammunition of various gauges.

I was beginning to wonder why I hadn't armed myself for this expedition.

Who would need this much firepower, and for what? I thought it might be interesting to check out the books on the shelves. I suspected that they were not likely to be on the *New York Times* fiction best-sellers list. It was at that moment, as I took a step toward the shelves, that my brain was napalmed. Someone had whacked me at the base of my skull with something blunt and solid. I somehow clung on to consciousness, and tried to turn to see my attacker, but a cloth soaked in something sweet and sickly was pressed against my face.

What happened next was almost pleasant at first. I was rushing through a cartoon desert on a rocket sled, saguaro cactuses flashing by. I'd been through this before when I was thirteen years old, and had my appendix removed. I knew what to expect. I'd seen my share of Wile E. Coyote and Road Runner movies, and felt strangely fulfilled as I shot off the edge of the cliff and fell endlessly into the canyon below.

NINE

When I came to, my head felt like a hockey puck after a
date with Bobby Hull. I was flat on my back on the floor in a pool
of sunlight. Someone must have raised the blinds, probably on pur-
pose, knowing it would be like throwing acid in my face. I squeezed
my eyes shut, but it didn't help. The light burned through my eyelids. I wondered why I wasn't dead. If someone wants to inflict that
kind of misery, why don't they just chill you and be done with it?
Either these people were sadists or amateurs.

The events leading up to my condition came back slowly. I
managed to sit up and feel the back of my head. My hair was mat-
ted with blood. There was a bump on my forehead, too. I must
have hit it on the edge of the table as I fell. I clenched my teeth
and tried to check out my surroundings. One of my molars was
cracked. Every muscle in my neck and shoulders screamed for
mercy, and I saw that the room—which was slowly spinning—
was now completely empty. Everything had gone: the guns, the
ammo, the telephone, the table, the chairs, the television, the
books, the coffeemaker, even the mattresses. I guess whoever it
was that zapped me didn't want me to get too comfortable. But

he or she or they had folded my leather jacket neatly on the floor beside me, and nothing was missing from my wallet.

I lay on my back some more, using the jacket as a pillow, and tried to will some life back into my body. Eventually, I was able to stand up and move around. I checked out the space on foot. There was a door at the back, which opened onto a little bathroom containing a sink and a toilet. There was nothing in there either—not so much as a toothpick or a Kotex—but at least I could splash water on my face, wash some of the blood out of my hair, and relieve myself. Then I headed downstairs, checking out every floor as I went. None of the doors were locked. All of the rooms were empty. It was as if someone wanted to be sure that I got a good look at the whole building so that I could see that it was as clean as a whistle.

I stumbled out into the street and almost bumped into a guy in a Nehru jacket that had Filene's Basement written all over it. He asked if I was okay. I told him it was that time of the month, and asked if he was from around there.

"That's my brother-in-law's business next door," he said, "Slezak Buttons and Novelties."

I asked him if he knew anything about 137.

"Until a couple of years ago," he said, "that used to be the New York headquarters of Simon Jaffa Securities and Mortgages—a highly regarded business. They relocated to Sarasota. You don't get the respect around here anymore. The building's been empty since then, except some artist moved in a couple of months ago. But you don't take that serious. The way things are, you take any lease you can, but you can't sign a long-term lease with that kind. I hear this bunch moved out in the early hours this morning—probably without paying the rent. They had a truck and cleaned the place out."

"Did you see the truck?"

"Me? No. I heard this from a delivery guy."

"Do you know anything about the artist?" I asked. "Did you see him?"

"A loudmouth. I don't think he was living there, but he had a bunch of assistants. Some cute young girls. Some guys, too. You know the kind—long hair, bad hygiene. They might have been camping out here. It happens."

"Who owns the building?" I asked.

He shrugged.

"Who owns it? I couldn't say. The rental agent is Harry Zubin on Church Street. Probably he could tell you."

●　●　●

After that conversation, I checked out the Datsun. Its windshield was shattered and all four tires had been slashed. I'd have to deal with that later. In the meantime, I made my way on foot to Harry Zubin's office, cursing the Beatles for that *Good Day Sunshine* song, which kept ringing infuriatingly through my brain.

I didn't get to see Harry, but I did talk to a zaftig lady who described herself as his majordomo.

"If you're interested in leasing the Ladies Lane space," she told me, "you can talk directly to me. We are authorized to handle everything, and even a very short-term lease is open to discussion."

"Look," I said, "you don't have to worry about me going behind your back, but I've been burned once too often. I don't negotiate with anyone unless I know whose signature is on the title, or who carries the mortgage, or whatever the deal is. I'm interested in talking about a five-year lease on this property, so please, can we get real?"

I didn't know what the hell I was talking about, but I figured I sounded pretty convincing, given that there were Floor for Rent signs all over the neighborhood. The zaftig lady heard me out and asked me to bear with her for a few moments, then disappeared into an inner office. When she returned, she was smiling.

"We'll be glad to give you the information you request," she said, "if you could tell us a little more about your own business."

I got up and apologized for wasting her time.

"I can get this information from the city," I said. "It will mean I have to pay an assistant five bucks an hour to stand on line, but if that's the way it has to be…Or I can go to Jack Klein and see what properties he has available."

The zaftig lady saw the light.

"No point in getting upset about this," she said. "The property belongs to Donald and Shirley Baldridge. You've probably heard of Councilman Baldridge. You couldn't deal with nicer people."

That was better.

"I understand an artist—or a group of artists—has been renting the property," I said.

She shook her head.

"I don't know where you got that idea," she said. "There's been nobody in that building for a couple of years."

● ○ ●

I didn't call Mrs. Baldridge right away. First, I took a subway home, swallowed some Tylenol, showered, soaked in the tub for about half an hour, then took another shower. After all that, and a couple tokes of Mendocino Mauve, I was just about strong enough to scramble some eggs, which I helped down with a can of Ballantine Ale. I don't make a habit of drinking at breakfast, but sometimes the occasion calls for rules to be bent.

Feeling halfway normal, except for the bass drum throbbing inside my cerebellum, I called the car rental company and told them where they would find their vehicle. The woman at the other end of the line didn't sound pleased. Then I called Mrs. Baldridge. She answered the phone herself and recognized my voice.

"My husband's not here at the moment," she said. "Can I take a message?"

This was stated in a tone that told me that the Donald was definitely at home, probably perusing the minutes of the last meeting of the Sanitation & Waste Management Standing Committee as he scarfed down his Wheaties a few feet from the phone. I gave Mrs. Baldridge my office number, told her I'd be there in half an hour, and asked her to call me as soon as she could.

"I'm not sure that's possible," she said. "I've already given generously, as I'm sure you're aware."

I thanked her and told her it was urgent.

● ● ●

When I got to the office, I found a message from my other voluptuous matron, Mrs. Kravitz.

"I just received a phone call from someone who told me that I should not worry about Lydia. Lydia wanted me to know that she was safe. I tried to ask questions, but the girl hung up on me. She sounded young, but I didn't recognize the voice. Definitely not Andrea Marshall. I don't know what it means, but I suppose it's a relief, though my husband doesn't seem to think so. I thought I'd better let you know."

I told her not to get too excited.

"That may be good news, but there's no way of knowing for sure unless you speak directly to Lydia."

She made a noise as if she were about to put up a fight, then calmed down and asked if there were any new developments.

I told her I had some leads I was following. I don't think that made her happy, but she didn't push me. After she hung up, I tried again to call Mrs. Baldridge. There was no reply. Olga the masseuse stopped by to bum a cigarette. She was dressed the way she had been early that morning, and her shoulders were still stunning—but then I have a thing for freckles.

"You can't imagine the night I had." she said. "Some customers..."

"I had quite a workout myself," I told her.

"Poor boy, you look tense," she said, moving behind my back and placing her fingers on my neck. For five minutes, she kneaded my neck and shoulders. She was good. I told her I thought I was in love.

"Don't forget," she said. "A full-body rub any time you feel you need it. The first one's on me."

She left, and I was still waiting impatiently for Shirley Baldridge to call when the door opened and in walked Detective Campbell.

"Just a follow-up to our little conversation yesterday," he said, "the one about the report of a man with a gun."

"I guess you're a connoisseur of wild-goose chases," I suggested.

"I just like to tie up loose ends for my own satisfaction," said Campbell. "I like to be thorough. It's one of my few vices. I seem to remember you told me you don't carry heat, but that you have a thirty-eight at home. I forgot to ask, do you keep anything in the office?"

Campbell had a brain like one of those eighteenth-century Scottish thinkers I wrote a paper about at City College—David Hume or one of those dudes—empirical, skeptical, and a bit quirky. There was no point trying to bullshit my way out of this one.

"Yeah. There's a gun in my wall safe. D'you want to see it?"

Campbell shrugged.

"What model?" he asked.

"It's a Ruger—a thirty-eight. Smaller than the Smith & Wesson I keep at home, but they take the same ammo."

Campbell nodded.

"Too bad I didn't think to ask yesterday," he said. "But I happened to be passing, anyway."

Sure. His visit was as accidental as the summer solstice.

The phone rang. It was the West Indian help from the Baldridges' apartment. She asked me to hold for Mrs. Baldridge.

I told Campbell, "I have to take this."

He sat tight and took out his pipe, as if he was about to settle in.

"It's confidential," I said.

Campbell nodded, and got up slowly.

"If you think of anything else," he said.

"About what?" I asked.

"About anything."

"You'll be the first to hear."

"By the way," he said, "that's a nasty bruise you have there on your forehead."

"Cab door," I said. "Some fleets operate with compacts these days."

"It's the pits," said Campbell.

Finally, he left, and a few seconds later, Mrs. Baldridge came on the line.

"Back for more already?" she said.

"I wish," I told her.

"Because, let's get this straight—I had a ball last night, but that was strictly a one-shot thing. That call-me-soon shtick was entirely for Donald's benefit. It worked, too. I wish you could have stayed for the fireworks."

"This is about something else."

"Okay, but make it snappy. He's working at home today—big speech to prepare. He's in the shower, but he doesn't make a meal out of it."

"Does 137 Ladies Lane mean anything to you? It's down in the loft district."

"The address doesn't mean anything," she said, "but Donald and I own some properties down there. He thought we'd make a killing when Robert Moses put the highway through. Moses owed Donald a favor, but now it looks like the highway deal is off, and we're stuck with worthless real estate. We've been talking about tearing the buildings down and converting them into parking lots. That way we get some income and cut out some property taxes. At least that's what Donald says."

"Do you know anything about renting 137 to artists?"

"I told you, the address means nothing to me. Our agent would handle that kind of crap. Harry Zubin."

"I talked to the sweetheart in Zubin's office. She didn't seem to know much about anything. When I heard it was your property, though, it made me wonder if your brother might somehow be involved."

"Why are you interested?" she asked.

"It's a long story."

"Are you some kind of cop?" she demanded. "Some kind of city snoop, or something to do with the feds? Is that why you were hanging around last night? Is Donald in some kind of trouble? Oh, my God!"

It passed through my mind that it might be good for her to chew on that possibility for a while.

"We need to talk," I said. "Face-to-face."

"Oh, my God!" she said again. "Today is difficult. It's the science fair at my kid's school. I have to be there."

"What about this evening?"

"This evening I'm going to an opening at the Museum of Modern Art."

"With the future mayor?"

"No, he hates those things. Says they're full of fags and phonies. I'm going with Julian, my decorator."

We arranged to rendezvous at the Modern, at the foot of the escalator, at eight o'clock. I heard her say, "You're dripping on the parquet, Donald..." Then she hung up.

● ● ●

I thought it was about time to give Gabriel Kravitz an update. After all, he was paying the bills. On the other hand, what could I tell him? I doubted that he would see the fact that I'd been hit over the head, shot at, and nearly mangled beneath a train as good value for his money, since so far, nothing had brought any tangible results. In my head, I prepared a heavily edited version of recent events and called the direct line to his office. In companies like Kravitz Developments, Inc., the direct line is never really direct. The call was answered by a hard-nosed assistant, the sort of woman who provides her boss with his first and last lines of defense, even if he is facing charges of embezzlement, fraud, abduction, aggravated sodomy, and ripping off the money from the church bake sale.

"Mr. Kravitz can't talk to anyone," she said.

I gave her my name and told her that Mr. Kravitz had told me I could call at any time.

"You still can't talk to him," she said. "He was called away on unexpected business. He did leave your name, however, and said that if you called I was to tell you he would contact you later."

Once again, I was stumped by what to do next, and this time, I fell back on an old standby. I would go to the New York Public Library newspaper room, which in those days was a sizable freestanding building in Hell's Kitchen, a warehouse full of millions of newspapers from all over the world, some on microfilm, some bound between boards, precious depositaries of public chicanery and private indiscretion. I liked the ones that had survived as newsprint for their feel and smell, the gritty aroma of history they gave off. Sometimes, when I was getting nowhere with an investigation, I would order back issues from the twenties or thirties, of the *Chicago Tribune* or the *Pittsburgh Sun-Telegraph*, just to read the Sunday comics sections. More often though, I would try to research something associated with the case I was working on, however peripheral it might seem. This at least provided backstory and gave me a sense of sending out feelers that might somehow connect with something useful. Once in a while, one of them did.

On this occasion, I started with the *New York Times*, using the article index to reference Jerry Pedrosian. There were half a dozen reviews of solo exhibitions by hard-line scribes like Hilton Kramer and John Canaday—none of them telling me anything I didn't know—and several mentions of his participation in museum shows, or other group exhibitions. His name appeared among those present at a handful of social events, and then there was one mention that was much more interesting. In the summer of 1960, when Jack Kennedy was running for president, Pedrosian had been the spokesman for a group of avant-garde artists, writers, actors, filmmakers and musicians who noisily interrupted a speech by JFK at the Brooklyn Navy Yard to demand that the candidate state his position on government support for the arts. The article suggested that Kennedy had handled the situation with charm and humor, and had won over the young would-be radicals.

I checked this story out in other New York papers and got lucky, coming up with a photograph of a smiling Jack Kennedy shaking hands with Jerry Pedrosian against the background of a placard that announced, "Kennedy—Our Next President." Jerry looked like he'd just hit the jackpot on *Name that Tune.*

I made a photocopy of the picture and, feeling pleased with myself without much reason, decided to head back to my apartment to get some sleep before I put myself together for the MoMA opening. I walked to the Port Authority Bus Terminal, descended to subway level, and boarded a downtown C train. Just before the doors closed, three kids boarded, two girls and a boy in their late teens or early twenties. The girls looked like typical art students, in men's shirts and jeans, the boy looked more like a hippie, with a headband and a mustache, and wore one of those suede fringed vests that were considered cool at the time. They sat down directly across from me, so I had a lot of time to study them. There was no reason to do so, but they looked vaguely familiar. The boy looked at me once then looked quickly away. I decided to stare, and got the impression they were deliberately ignoring me.

Only when I got off the train at 14th Street did I realize where I'd seen those kids before. They were the self-righteous trio that had been arguing politics with Martin Wolfe at the Mafioso bar on Prince Street. On the face of it, it was comfortably within the laws of probability that I would find myself on the same train with them, since they obviously hung out together, and most likely crashed somewhere downtown. Like 137 Ladies Lane maybe?

I told myself I was putting two and two together and coming up with the title of a Fellini film. Even so, I was spooked.

TEN

The Museum of Modern Art was a lot cozier in those days. Sometimes, on a weekday morning, you could visit the Matisse room and find yourself alone with a priceless harem of swooning odalisques and naked houris, undisturbed by parties of lost souls drifting through the galleries at a pace determined by the audio pods clamped to their ears. Openings were another matter, and on evenings when some long-awaited survey or retrospective was unveiled, crowds swarmed through the building, sipping wine, riding the escalators, or clustering around familiar bronzes in Philip Johnson's sculpture garden, eyeballing celebrities.

I don't recall what show opened that evening. I arrived a little before eight, early enough to take in the crowd, which was the usual mix of tuxedoed Brahmins, Park Avenue matrons, and haute bourgeois hangers-on. Saint Andy was already in attendance, surrounded by his usual motley entourage, and sporting a shawl-lapelled tuxedo jacket with jeans and sneakers.

I found Shirley Baldridge at the appointed place and time. She had already dumped her decorator and was all mine. Not that she was particularly pleased to see me.

"So I fucked a detective!" she said, loud enough for the woman next to her to turn and stare.

I took her arm and led her to a quieter spot overlooking the sculpture court.

"Just so you know," she said. "I'm wearing a chastity belt."

I doubted the truth of that, but she did have on a severe outfit with a boxy jacket that gave off none of the signals she had been flashing the evening before.

"Okay, I'm a detective," I said, "but I'm not with any government agency. I'm not after your husband, or your family."

That calmed her down a bit.

"I'm a self-employed private eye trying to earn a buck. I'm working on a missing persons case, and your brother may be involved. How involved, I don't know. To the best of my knowledge, he's done nothing illegal. Also to the best of my knowledge, the police are not involved, though I'm not one hundred percent sure of that. What I told you last night is true. I do know Jerry, though not particularly well. To be honest, I don't like him, and he doesn't like me."

"What have you got against him?" she said.

"If you'd asked me that question a couple of days ago, I would have said we're oil and water, and left it that. Now I can be more specific. I just found out he slept with my ex-wife—while I was still married to her."

Mrs. Baldridge laughed—a truncated snort of a laugh. She somehow didn't seem as appealing tonight.

"This is getting incestuous," she said.

I agreed.

"When was the last time you saw Jerry?" I asked.

"Months ago," she said. "I told you, we don't get along. But he's probably here tonight. He doesn't like to miss these things."

"I doubt it," I told her. "Nobody's seen him for days."

"So maybe he took a trip. So what?"

"The reason I called you about the building on Ladies Lane is because there were some artists in there recently, even though your agent doesn't know about it. I'd like to know if one of them was Jerry."

"He's got his own place," she said. "Jerry has money."

"Still—I have a feeling he might have been there. Does he have a key to that place?"

"Why would I give him a key?" she asked.

Then she paused.

"You know what, he might have a key. I don't get along with Jerry, but strangely enough, Donald does. It's weird. They have nothing in common, but for some perverse reason, they hit it off. Probably because they both have their brains below their belts. I remember now. When we bought those properties, Donald asked Jerry to keep an eye on them. It made sense, I guess, since he lives a couple of blocks away. Yeah, he might have a key."

"But you've no reason to think he's been using it?"

She shrugged.

"Hey, we're talking about Jerry. He wouldn't bother to tell me. Not that I could care less. But now tell me something, who is this missing person? Jerry?"

"It's a girl."

"So he's shacked up with some tart. And who are you working for?"

"Her father."

"Daddy's little darling having it off with the big bad artist? How old?"

"Eighteen."

"That's young, even for Jerry, but at least it's legal. I can see why the father would be pissed, though. Anyone I might know?"

I ignored the question and pulled out the newspaper photograph I had Xeroxed that afternoon—the one of Jerry with Jack Kennedy—and showed it to her.

She laughed.

"Where did you get that?"

"You've seen it before?"

"Sure, we were still talking in those days. Look at the expression on Jerry's face. He was smitten. He'd been totally against Kennedy till that day—talked about Joe Kennedy and the mob planning to steal the election from the American people. I don't remember who Jerry was for—probably some anarchist libertarian—but it sure wasn't Kennedy. Being against everything is Jerry's specialty. He was righteously pissed about Vietnam, about civil rights, about everything. Like I told you, he spent too much time with our aunt Ida, the crazy old woman. Jerry wanted to change the world, but then Kennedy shook his hand and gave him that big phony smile. Poof! Jerry was in love. He campaigned for Kennedy, went to Washington for the inauguration. And then came the Bay of Pigs, and the Missile Crisis. Jerry felt betrayed, poor baby. He actually tried to go to Havana. Of course there was no way he could get there, but Fidel became his new hero."

"I had no idea Jerry was that serious about politics."

"You call that serious? I call it naïve. He's the type who talks a good game, but doesn't bother to register to vote. Anyway, it's all about having a hot line to pitch to girls. He votes with his testicles."

At this point, Mrs. Baldridge was looking away from me, over my shoulder.

"There's a woman staring at you," she said.

I turned to look and saw Marion Kravitz. Given that she was a collector, her presence at the opening was hardly a surprise. She flashed me a nervous smile.

"Do I detect a rival?" asked Mrs. Baldridge.

"Someone I have some business with," I said.

"And you don't have business with me?"

"Look, I'm sorry. Can you hang around for a couple of minutes? I have to speak to this woman."

"Why don't you introduce us?" said Mrs. Baldridge, upping the sarcasm. "Maybe we can make it a threesome."

I ignored this and crossed over to Marion Kravitz, who was wearing a black cocktail dress not unlike the one Mrs. Baldridge had worn the previous evening. She looked good, if it's possible to look good and thoroughly stressed out at the same time.

"Who's that?" she asked.

"A woman I know."

"I have to talk to you," she said.

"I'm right here."

"Can we go somewhere else?" she said. "That woman is watching us."

I led her out into the sculpture court.

"I want you to drop the case," she said.

I hadn't seen that coming.

"Did you hear me? I want you to drop the case," she repeated.

"Lydia has been found?"

"No, but I'm sure she's okay."

"Because of that message you received?"

"Partly…"

"There's something else?"

"Not exactly. It's just a feeling. If she's with Jerry Pedrosian, he's not going to let her come to any harm."

"Why are you so sure?"

"I know Jerry—at least I knew him. I told you that. I used to collect his work. We socialized occasionally. He's wild, but he wouldn't let anything happen to Lydia."

Her earnestness was painful.

"And does your husband agree?"

"I haven't spoken to him about it yet."

"Is he here tonight?"

She shook her head.

"Do you mind telling me how I can get hold of him? Because you may be the girl's mother, Mrs. Kravitz, but he's the one who hired me for this gig. My contractual obligations are to him."

"I don't know where he is. He was called out of town."

"That's what his minions told me. Has he been in touch?"

Again, she shook her head.

"Is that unusual?"

"Well, a little. But he's a businessman. Sometimes he just jumps on a plane and flies to Seattle, or Munich, or wherever."

"Without letting you know?"

She seemed to have no answer to that.

"Do you suspect he's in some kind of trouble?"

I was playing a hunch.

"Not exactly."

"What does 'not exactly' mean?"

Again, no answer.

"What do you think is going on, Mrs. Kravitz?"

"To tell you the truth, I have no idea."

Tears welled up in her eyes and she looked faint. I helped her to a bench.

"Stay here," I told her. "I have to let my friend know that I'll be tied up for a while, then we'll get out of here and we'll go somewhere quiet where we can talk. I'll be right back."

Mrs. Baldridge was nowhere to be seen. I figured that at this point in the proceedings Mrs. Kravitz was my primary concern anyway, so I hurried back to the sculpture court. The bench was empty. Feeling frustrated and foolish, I went back inside and scanned the crowd. There was no sign of either of them, but near the top of the escalator, ascending to the upper floors, was an ethereal-looking girl in a white dress, with long blond hair. She looked back in my direction, then disappeared.

ELEVEN

I hung around at the opening for a while, hoping that the blond girl, or one of the women might materialize out of the crowd. No such luck. I took a taxi to my office in the hope that one of them might have called in with an explanation. Bubkes. I walked to Max's and had a drink at the bar. Being there jogged my memory. When I had spoken to Doug Mills at Max's a couple of evenings earlier, he had told me that Jerry Pedrosian's red Pontiac was parked in the lot next to the bodega on West Broadway. I should have followed up on that before. I took a cab down to SoHo and checked out the parking lot through the chain-link fence. No red Pontiac. I went into the bodega and talked to Hector, the *patrón*.

Did he know Jerry Pedrosian? Hector said he knew a lot of people, but he didn't always know their names. Did he know the guy who drove the red Pontiac that parked in the lot next door? Oh, *that* Jerry? Sure he knew that Jerry. That Jerry bought cigarettes and coffee and Heinekens and Milky Way bars, and sometimes he cashed a check for five or ten dollars. They never bounced. That Jerry was an okay guy. Had that Jerry been around lately? Hector hadn't seen that Jerry lately, but he had seen the car. Someone—not Jerry—was driving it toward Canal Street. When had that been? Hector couldn't say. Maybe earlier that day, maybe the day before.

● ○ ●

I walked home on Bleecker Street. As soon as I opened the door to my apartment, I had a feeling that something was out of whack. I turned on the overhead light and discovered Andrea Marshall in my bed. The sheets were pulled up to her chin, but I was pretty sure that underneath them she wasn't decked out in a whole lot of livery, a notion that was borne out by the little pile of female clothing on the floor alongside the bed. She smiled at me, fetchingly, and petted Samba, who was curled up on her chest, purring.

I decided to take the laid-back option, sat down on the rocker where I threw my threads at night, and lit a cigarette.

"How did you get in?" I asked.

"Easy," she said. "I rang all the front door bells and a nice little queer with glasses came down and opened the door."

That would have been Ethan, who lived on the floor above me.

"I explained how I was your niece from Poughkeepsie, and that I was staying with you while I did college interviews, but I had locked myself out. So he let me in."

I could have called Ethan to check the story, but it sounded plausible. Everyone in the building had keys to everyone else's apartment.

"He didn't have any questions about your story?"

"I told him I'd tried to reach you at your office on Union Square. I think that convinced him."

"How did you know I have an office on Union Square?"

"You told me the other night. You said I could always leave a message there because there's a machine. You gave me a number."

"And to what do I owe this unexpected pleasure?"

"I came to apologize for running out on you the other night. My boyfriend Jonathon dragged me away. He's not really my boyfriend, but he likes to think he is. I'd asked him to keep an eye on me because I didn't know what was going to happen. I didn't tell him anything about Lydia, of course. I told him it was about buying some grass, and I told him to stay out of sight. While you were in the bathroom with the gun, he came to the door of the restaurant, and he was kind of mad. He said he knew that something was going on between you and me and he was going to confront you. I told him not to be stupid, but he wouldn't listen. I didn't want any trouble, especially with the gun and all, so I went with him to keep him quiet. That's how it happened. Honest…"

This was all said in a girlish rush, quite unlike her more confrontational manner on the earlier occasion. Except, come to think of it, that moment when she had turned on the Little Girl Lost look under the lamppost. If the boyfriend had seen that, he might have thought he had cause for alarm. Now, having protested her innocence, Andrea looked at me as if eagerly anticipating my next contribution to the dialogue.

"And while you were waiting for me tonight," I said, "you got tired, took off all your clothes, and crawled into my bed—just like Snow White and Goldilocks and Little Red Riding Hood and all that fairy-tale jailbait."

"They didn't take off their clothes, did they?" she said.

"That's what their attorneys would like you to believe," I told her. "Anyway, what are you doing in my bed?"

"I wanted to surprise you," she said.

"Congratulations. You managed that."

"And I wanted to show you I was sorry for what happened."

Now the look was contrite, in a kittenish kind of way that wouldn't have fooled Samba.

"It looks to me like the apology you have in mind doesn't exactly fit the crime."

She giggled.

Deep down, a little voice told me, "Get her out of here before you start telling her about your collection of Buddy Holly 78s." The fact remained, though, that this tantalizing bundle of enzymes, X chromosomes, and hormonal signifiers undoubtedly had answers to questions that had a bearing on the case I had been hired to solve. Another voice from somewhere in the left side of the brain argued, "Take it easy. You're supposed to be a man of the universe, able to handle any kind of situation a little bimbo like this can throw at you. Make her sing. Just don't lay a finger on her."

Easy for the left side of the brain to say.

"So that's all you're here for?" I said. "To apologize?"

"That's right," she said, kittenish again, though there was something counterfeit about her come-and-get-me purr. I had the feeling that she hadn't done anything remotely like this before. Still, she kept trying.

"Why don't you sit over here?" she said, patting the edge of the bed.

"First, a couple of questions. Have you heard from Lydia, or seen her, since we last talked?"

She shook her head.

"Where have you been since you disappeared from the restaurant the other night?"

"Well, I had to go back to Jonny's place. I had to show him— you know..."

"You had to apologize?"

She giggled.

"You've got a dirty mind," she said.

"So you apologized to Jonny," I said, "and where have you been since then?"

"Mostly in my apartment."

"I tried you there several times. You never picked up."

"Well, a girl doesn't just sit by the phone all day long waiting for Prince Charming. I'm in school. I had classes."

I took a gamble.

"I checked with school. You haven't attended class in two days."

She was clearly unnerved by this.

"You don't even know where I go to school," she said, petulant now.

"Sure I do. I know that Lydia tried to get you to apply to Teddington, but you chose NYU."

"The school doesn't give out private information," she said.

"Depends who you know," I told her. "In my line of work, you get to know a lot of people in useful positions at places like NYU."

"So what if I took time off?" she said, rattled.

"What did you do with your time off?"

"None of your business," she said.

Now the expression was wounded pride.

"Maybe it is my business. You've lied to me at least once, so how can I be sure you weren't hanging out with Lydia?"

"I don't know where she is."

"Did Jerry Pedrosian send you here tonight?"

Now she mimed exasperation.

"I don't *know* Jerry Pedrosian. You know that. I've only met him a couple of times."

"So who sent you?"

"Nobody sent me. I came because I wanted to see you."

"Oh, yeah—I forgot. You wanted to apologize."

"Not anymore," she said angrily.

With that, she threw off the covers and sat up.

"Good idea," I said, trying not to appear too interested in what was now revealed. In reality, despite my display of self-restraint, I had not been able to suppress the instinct to fantasize about what I would find if I had crawled under the sheets with her, and had not been far off the mark.

"Get dressed and get out of here," I told her.

I thought there was a better chance of that happening if I wasn't hanging around pretending not to be a voyeur, so I went to the kitchen and poured myself a drink. When I came back, Andrea was seated on the edge of the bed. She was still stark naked except for cotton panties.

"I am legal, you know," she said.

"You're what?"

"I'm eighteen years old. Nineteen next week. You wouldn't get into trouble."

She looked down at her body, coyly, as if asking me to agree that it was not entirely unpalatable. Again, I had the feeling that there was something a shade counterfeit about this. It was like being at a rehearsal of a show in which the lead actress hasn't quite got under the skin of the character yet. Andrea had the physical attributes to become a seductress, but the experience wasn't there, though under other circumstances it would have been easy to overlook that little detail.

"That's it," I said. "I'm getting out of here right now. I'm going to walk around a couple of blocks, and when I get back, if you're still here, I'm going to throw you out onto the street, even if you don't have a stitch on."

I left and walked to Abingdon Square Park, from where I had a view of my front door. Andrea emerged after about ten minutes and headed east on 12th Street. I followed at a discreet distance. At Bleecker she turned south, then headed east again on Christopher. She stopped at Village Cigars, probably to buy cigarettes, then crossed 7th Avenue to the Sheridan Square newsstand, where she bought a magazine. I waited to see if she would head down into the subway, and she did just that. I ran down the steps at another entrance, on the west side of 7th Avenue, just in time to see her push through the turnstile and head for the uptown platform. I felt in my pocket and found I was out of tokens. I would have vaulted the turnstile, but there was a traffic cop right there. People have been shot for less. By the time I had purchased a token, I could hear an uptown train pulling into the station, and by the time I reached the platform it was just a pattern of lights disappearing into the tunnel.

The frustration and anticlimax made me realize how beat I was. I returned to my place and drank the scotch I had poured for myself while Andrea was there. I tried to come up with a plan for the next day, but my brain refused to cooperate. It was more interested in conjuring up the image of Andrea, sitting there naked on the edge of my bed. I tried watching TV to distract myself. Ethel Merman on Johnny Carson. A George O'Brien oater on Channel Eleven.

I undressed and got into bed. The smell of the sheets was intoxicating. Samba jumped up beside me and purred.

TWELVE

I had a feeling I should know much more about Andrea Marshall, so the next morning I decided to pay a surprise visit to her parents. I had found out from my pal Mike at the *Post* that they were both writers, so it was a safe bet they worked at home, but I called first to make sure someone was there. When a woman with a Seven Sisters accent answered, I said, "Sorry, wrong number."

Seldon Marshall was an author of action yarns. Starting before Pearl Harbor, he had made his name churning out formulaic short stories and serials for the *Saturday Evening Post* and other weeklies, then in the 1950s, he had written *The Last Sortie*, which was considered a minor classic of World War II fiction. Since then, it had been mostly downhill but a couple of his stories had been made into movies. Alyson Marshall was responsible for a string of historical novels, typically set in eighteenth-century England or Colonial America, that were fixtures in the middle range of the *New York Times* best-sellers list. The Marshalls' apartment was on West End Avenue in an ugly mansion block just above 72nd Street. The doorman was ugly, too, but looked like he might be amenable to a bribe. With that in mind, I had bought a bouquet of roses at a florist on Broadway. Now I waved a five-dollar bill in the doorman's face and said, "I'm Mrs. Marshall's agent. It's her birthday and I want to surprise her."

"I thought her birthday was last month," said Wesley. His name was on a plastic tag pinned to his jacket.

"That's right," I said, "but this is her official birthday. Writers have real birthdays and official birthdays, like the Queen of England. It's for publicity purposes."

Wes said he wished he had two birthdays. I said, "Me, too. What was that apartment number again?"

I took the elevator to the eleventh floor, tossed the roses into the garbage chute, found the door marked *F*, and rang the bell. It was answered by Andrea, who did a double take worthy of Oliver Hardy.

I was kind of surprised to see her, too.

"You're not going to tell them, are you?" she whispered.

"Don't worry," I assured her. "I'm not here to make waves."

"Who is it, dear?" a woman called from somewhere inside the apartment.

"It's the man I was telling you about," Andrea called back. "Mr. Novalis. The investigator who's looking for Lydia."

It was another of those sprawling Upper West Side apartments, with mellow woodwork and a lot of rooms. Andrea, who was dressed in a demure shirtwaist dress, ushered me into a big, brightly lit sitting room, furnished with a mix of low-key British antiques and comfortable soft chairs upholstered in expensive-looking floral prints. It made me think of 1930s photographs—Ethel Barrymore at home, or Mr. and Mrs. Cole Porter in the sunroom of their rented villa at Antibes. Alyson Marshall sat in one of the easy chairs, a notebook resting on her lap. She wore a white silk blouse with a pleated cream-colored skirt, and it was easy to see where Andrea's looks came from, though Mrs. Marshall's demeanor in no way betrayed the fact that she was the author of bodice rippers tailored to the fantasies of pre-feminist housewives.

I guessed Mrs. Marshall was in her early forties. Her husband, who appeared to be close to twenty years her senior, sat to her right, in a motorized wheelchair. I later learned that he had suffered a serious back injury in the war while crash-landing an Avenger on the deck of a heaving escort carrier during the buildup to the Battle of Okinawa. He was a big man, in a tweed suit and a dark shirt, a polka-dot bow tie, and brown suede brogues. An artfully folded breast pocket handkerchief matched the bow tie. Seldon Marshall seemed somehow overdressed for a man in a wheelchair in his own home.

He greeted me with the kind of curt nod often favored by strong silent types in his novels. Mrs. Marshall was more forthcoming.

"How nice of you to stop by," she said. "Mr. Novalis, is it?"

"Alex Novalis. I was in the neighborhood."

"I wonder why Wes didn't announce you?" she wondered.

"He was having trouble with the intercom," I told her.

"We'll have to look into that," she said. "Very annoying. Will you remind me to report it to the board, Sel?"

Her husband made a noise like a seal swallowing a mackerel tossed by a zookeeper.

I glanced at Andrea, who looked about as comfortable as a poodle in a cage full of pit bulls. Alyson Marshall looked at her, too, a tight smile on her lips, then turned back to me.

"Andrea has indeed mentioned you," she said. "You are the person who the Kravitzes have hired?"

She managed to make "person" sound like a dirty word. "Hired" also had a less-than-savory ring to it.

"I've been engaged to find Lydia," I said. "I've talked to Andrea, and she's been very helpful."

"I presume you mean that in a purely idiomatic way," said Mrs. Marshall, "since, of course, she knows nothing about Lydia's disappearance."

"That's precisely what she told me," I said.

Mrs. Marshall looked at Andrea again.

"Why don't you go to your room, dear?" she said.

She spoke to her daughter as if she were a four-year-old. Andrea disappeared, gratefully, as if she'd been let off with a ten-dollar fine and community service.

There was a transition. I was offered tea or coffee. I declined.

"I'm afraid this has been a bit of a wasted journey for you," said Mrs. Marshall.

"I thought," I said, "that you and your husband might be able to offer some perspective that could have escaped Andrea."

Mrs. Marshall sighed. Mr. Marshall rolled his eyes.

"I'm afraid we have nothing to add," she said.

"No idea where Lydia might be?"

"It's been some time seen we've seen her."

"But she and Andrea have remained in touch?"

"Until recently, unfortunately."

"Why, unfortunately?"

"Andrea's a good girl," said Mrs. Marshall.

I had been waiting for that.

"When she and Lydia first became friends," she continued, "we thought it was an appropriate relationship. We continued to think so until two—perhaps three—years ago. I hate to speak ill of people, but poor Lydia changed. Almost overnight she became a different person, what I can only call a bad influence. I know that adolescents go through these phases, but with Lydia it was something more. Again, I'm reluctant to say such a thing, but it was as if she had the mark of evil on her. You might find that novelistic, but then I am a novelist and I honor my craft. I don't know if you believe in evil, but to me it is something very real, something tangible that curdles the soul. Lydia has that quality of curdling the soul. What makes it so much worse is that she appears to be such an innocent. An angel. It's an illusion."

"Can you be more specific?" I asked.

Mrs. Marshall shook her head.

"So many things," she said, "but I don't want this to be a case of *j'accuse.* Perhaps there are mitigating circumstances. Her mother, for example. Marion Kravitz. We liked her well enough at first. She appeared to be the model parent, elected to the school's council, active in a variety of activities. But then…"

"Then?"

"It's not appropriate for me to discuss. My problems with Marion are irrelevant to the matter at hand, except to the extent that they lead me to cite Lydia as an example of a bad seed. I'm sorry about the girl's disappearance, and I hope that nothing terrible has happened to her, such as you read about in the newspapers, but if she's out of Andrea's life—and Andrea assures me she is—then I can only give thanks to the Almighty. One thing you can be sure of, anything you hear from Andrea is the truth. She's one of those people who is incapable of not telling the truth. And now, if you'll excuse us, both my husband and I have strict work schedules that must be adhered to."

"And let me add," said Seldon Marshall in a hoarse whisper, "if you drag my daughter into this filthy mess, I will personally see to it that you never have children as long as you live. I may be in a wheelchair, but to a marine, that's a minor inconvenience. I can still kill you with my bare hands. And when it's over, you'll thank me."

Mrs. Marshall gave me another of her tight smiles, and called out, "Andrea, your guest is leaving."

"Guest" seemed like an odd choice of words.

Andrea appeared, looking shell-shocked.

"I'll see you out," she said.

I said my polite farewells to her parents, and followed her to the apartment's front door.

"Give me an hour," she whispered. "I can't run out immediately or they'll be suspicious. There's a coffee shop on Broadway called Benny's. Meet me there."

● ○ ●

I spotted her as she crossed the northbound lanes from Broadway's center divider where old ladies out of a Sholem Aleichem story sat on benches dreaming of their final destination, which for the time being was probably Zabar's. Even in that demure shirtwaist number, Andrea looked delectable—one of those girls who can't help projecting sensuality.

I had been sitting near the window so I would see her, but now we moved to a booth in the back with more privacy. Andrea ordered chamomile tea and a muffin.

"God, you gave me a scare," she said. "Do you know what they'd have done to me if you had mentioned a word about last night?"

I told her I could imagine.

"I presume they gave you the Andrea's-a-good-girl routine?"

"Incapable of telling a lie."

"They're kind of old school."

"I'm amazed they let you have your own apartment."

"It's my great-aunt's. She lives in Mexico and only uses the place a couple of weeks a year. She specifically made it available to me—a graduation gift. It would have been hard for them to refuse."

I asked what she wanted from me now, while wondering why I somehow felt empathy for this girl who had given me the runaround and then pulled a Lolita stunt. I also wondered if empathy was the right word.

"Well, first of all," she said, "let me apologize for last night. What I did was really dumb."

"Let's not get into the apologies again," I told her.

She blushed.

"I'll tell you what really happened," she said.

Her tone was down-to-earth. I wanted to think it was believable.

"Most of what I told you that first evening was true. Lydia came to my apartment last weekend, we went to a party, she went off with Jerry, I found the gun in her bag. All that's the way it happened, and it's also true that I haven't seen her since. The part about Jonathon being jealous and dragging me away from the restaurant, that was true, too. He said he'd seen the way I looked at you and he knew that something was going on. Anyway, I spent most of the next day at his place because I was scared and didn't know what to do or where to go. I didn't go back to my apartment until yesterday, early afternoon. Jerry Pedrosian was waiting for me."

"In your apartment?"

"No. He was waiting on a stoop nearby."

"How did he know you'd be there at that time?"

"Okay, I told you I haven't seen Lydia, and that's true. And I haven't spoken to her, but she gave me a number where I could leave messages for her. She wanted me to keep calling in to leave word of where I would be. I called in when I was going to meet you that first time. I called to let her know I was at Jonny's, and I told her you had the gun. I called to tell her I was headed back to my own apartment. You get the picture. If Lydia was with Pedrosian, or if he was in touch with her, he had the means of knowing where I would be pretty much all the time."

"Can I have that number?"

She fished it out of her purse and I copied it into my notebook.

"It's an answering service," she said. "When you call, you can hear a bunch of women taking calls in the background."

"So Jerry waylaid you…"

"Yeah. We sat on a bench near the Women's House of Detention, with all the whores screaming at us out of the windows. Jerry had a guy with him, like a bodyguard—red hair, army fatigues—walking up and down on the sidewalk like he was some kind of a lookout. Jerry told me what he wanted me to do. He said that Lydia was in danger because of the investigation that her father had started. He wouldn't tell me what kind of danger, but he said that you had to be neutralized. That was the word he used—neutralized. If I was truly Lydia's friend, he said, and if I really wanted to help her, I would worm my way into your confidence and find out what you knew."

"So he suggested you seduce me for starters?"

Andrea blushed again.

"I asked him how I was supposed to go about that. He looked me over and grinned and said he was sure I'd think of something. He said that with someone like you it was the best way. Said it was surefire. The problem was I've never done anything like that. I asked myself, how do things like that happen in the movies? I mean, maybe like that scene in *The Graduate,* but flip-flopped? You know? Younger girl, older guy. Not that you're as old as Mrs. Robinson, of course…"

"Thanks a lot."

"But I guess I couldn't cut it," she said. "Lydia would have known what to do. She always had a thing about older guys, like Jerry. She says they're more interesting. I see guys like that looking at me on the street. I know what those looks mean, but…"

Again, the irresistible blush.

"I just didn't know what to do next," she said.

"No need to apologize," I said, which made her giggle. I had a sense that there had been a useful hookup of neurons inside her brain since this conversation had started. I would have liked to dwell on the consequences down the road, but it was time to get back to business.

"Did Pedrosian tell you what he wanted you to find out about me?"

"He wanted to know how much you knew about him and Lydia."

I didn't buy that. Much too vague.

"Do you have any idea what's going on between them—Lydia and Jerry Pedrosian?"

She shook her head.

"Why are they in hiding?"

"I wish I knew. I don't like it that Lydia's disappeared."

"And what's the deal with the gun?" I asked. "Why did she have a gun in her bag?"

"I haven't the faintest," said Andrea. "All I can tell you is that ever since she met Jerry Pedrosian, she's been different. It's not that we stopped being friends, but it hasn't been the same. She's been very secretive. It used to be that we told each other about everything. And I mean *everything*. When she slept with a guy, she would give me so much detail I would almost feel like I'd slept with him myself. But not Jerry."

"So she was a bad girl, just like your mother says?"

"I guess we both were a little naughty, but she was naughtier."

I decided to try something from out of left field.

"And how did she get pregnant?"

Andrea was shocked.

"How do you know about that?"

"Lydia's mother told me."

"Marion fucking Kravitz is a bitch, but I didn't think she was that big a bitch! About her own daughter! Lydia would kill her!"

A waitress with glasses on a silver chain asked Andrea to keep her voice down. Andrea glared into space.

"You don't have to tell me if you don't want to," I said.

"What's the difference," said Andrea. "Lydia told her mother that it was some French kid she'd met at the beach, but she told me it was a friend of her father's. Her mother took her to Aruba for an abortion."

"What did she tell her father?"

"Her father never knew about it."

"And Mrs. Kravitz said there was some problem with drugs."

Andrea hit the ceiling again.

"I'll strangle that woman! She had no right to tell you! Miss Ashley found one measly joint in my locker at school—half a joint, really—that Lydia and I had been sharing. Half a joint was how much was left after three days, smoking it one puff at a time. But it was a big scandal. Lydia owned up, but I got most of the blame. I nearly got thrown out of school."

"Which does help explain why Mrs. Kravitz doesn't see you as a steadying influence."

"Marion Kravitz doesn't like me. Ever since I started—uh—filling out, she's had it in for me."

"And what about Mr. Kravitz? You said once he was creepy."

"Did I say that?"

"That's what you said—a bit creepy."

She thought about it.

"He tries too hard to be helpful," she said. "He was always taking me and Lydia on trips. He would take us sailing, horseback riding. Once, when I was having problems with calculus, he offered to coach me. Mrs. Kravitz shot that idea down."

"I thought he wore the pants in the household?"

"Depends which pants you're talking about. There are pants for every occasion. Some of them come with lacey bits around the edges."

She said this with a certain tartness that I found odd.

"So how do you feel about Lydia now?" I asked.

"What do you mean? Lydia's my best friend."

"Yes, but she's the one who's getting you into all kinds of trouble. At least it seems that way to me."

Andrea looked dejected.

"She's still my friend. I don't want to see something bad happening to her."

"Would she be as worried if she thought something bad might happen to you?"

"Of course!"

I let her think about it for a while, then said, "Okay, I apologize. I thought for a while you were maybe the bad girl."

Tears welled up in Andrea's eyes again.

"If you'd taken advantage of my stupidity last night," she said, "you'd have been only the second guy I ever had sex with."

On that sobering thought, I changed the subject.

"So how are you supposed to report back to Pedrosian?" I asked.

"And what do I tell him?"

"Well, let's take those one at a time. Is there a plan with Pedrosian?"

"He said he would get in touch with me when I had something to tell him. I asked him how he would know when that was. He said, 'Don't worry—I'll know.' He made it sound kind of threatening. I feel he could show up at any moment, and then what?"

"If he really cares about Lydia's well-being, nothing bad is going to happen to you."

I thought of some of the things that had happened to me in the previous couple of days, and hoped I was right. Probably Pedrosian had known Andrea was in my apartment, and someone—either Pedrosian or somebody he had assigned—could have followed her when she left, though I had seen nothing suspicious as I trailed her.

"When you came uptown to your parents' apartment," I asked, "did you call the service and give your whereabouts?"

She shook her head.

"I was getting too freaked out."

That meant there was at least some chance Pedrosian did not know where Andrea was.

I laid it on the line for her.

"Do you really want to help Lydia?"

"Of course."

"Even though you know she's trouble—big trouble—and maybe *in* big trouble."

Andrea looked frightened. The truth was, I didn't know if Lydia really was big trouble, or in big trouble, or just a pain in the ass. And I still wasn't totally sure about Andrea, but I needed to get her reaction. She was confused.

"I don't want anything bad happening," she said.

"So are you willing to help me?"

"Help you how?"

"I'll have to figure that out, but remember you're our one possible bridge to Lydia, so if she is in trouble…"

"What do you want me to do?"

I told her to go back to her parents' apartment and stay put till I got in touch.

"Okay, but don't call their phone. I still have my own line in my old room."

She gave me the number.

"Who uses it now?" I asked. "Barbie and Ken?"

Andrea giggled. I liked that giggle a lot.

"Or call me at the office," I said. "You can always leave a message there."

THIRTEEN

So it was the good old good girl, bad girl scenario. The problem was that I wasn't sure which was which. Sitting there in the coffee shop with Andrea, I had wanted to believe everything she was telling me. Even after she was no longer there, I was pretty sure that the story she had just laid on me had many elements of truth to it, but it would take only one deliberately embedded lie to throw the whole thing off.

I stopped at a phone booth and called the number she had given me for the message service. When a woman answered, I asked, "Does this account belong to Jerry Pedrosian?" The woman said, "I'm sorry, sir, we can't give out that information."

Then I had a moment of inspiration.

"Does this account belong to Michigan J. Frog?"

I could tell by the woman's attempt to stifle a laugh that I had hit pay dirt. I was tempted to leave a message for Pedrosian, but that would compromise everything.

I took a subway downtown and went to my office to check my own messages. The third one was interesting. It was a male voice that I didn't recognize. Definitely not Pedrosian's, but I suspected the message had originated with him.

"We've been trying to warn you to mind your own business. Seems you're a bit thick, so let me spell it out for you. Lay off, or else."

● ● ●

My conversation with Andrea had made me curious about what kind of picture of Lydia I'd get if I contacted her school. I called Teddington and explained that I was the investigator who had been hired to look into Lydia's disappearance and was bounced around between administrative flacks until I finally spoke to an assistant dean.

"Lydia is a lovely girl," she said, "and extremely gifted. We thought she was rather quiet at first, but in fact, she's just extraordinarily self-possessed. She doesn't commit herself until she has something worth saying, if you understand me. If she has one failing, it's perhaps that she's a trifle over-confident."

"In what way?" I asked.

"How shall I put it? She's so determined to play a leadership role among her peers that she sometimes pushes a trifle too hard. But she's great fun and everyone here loves her."

"Does she have any special friends at Teddington?"

The woman paused.

"That's a difficult question to answer. She's been here just over one semester, and it takes time to forge those lifelong friendships that are among the cherished legacies of a school like Teddington. But Lydia's an extremely popular girl."

"What," I asked, "is her major?"

"At Teddington, we don't have majors. We believe in a broad, liberal education."

"Does Lydia have any areas in which she excels?"

"Oh, many areas. She tends to be at her best in fields that involve participation—debate for example. Last semester she was quite the star of a weeklong experimental workshop devoted to the subject of the interplay among art, politics, and society, emphasizing the potential role the artistic impulse can play in the community at large."

"That would have been Jerry Pedrosian's course?"

"Why yes. Do you know Mr. Pedrosian?"

"Lydia's father mentioned his course."

"I imagine he told you how much Lydia enjoyed it."

"He did say something of the sort. Could you tell me more about that course? What was Mr. Pedrosian's point of view?"

"I didn't personally attend any of the sessions, but my understanding is that he took the viewpoint that art should play an essentially subversive role, so that the social contract does not ossify into a rigid set of rules."

"And how does the school feel about that point of view?"

"You must understand," said the vice-dean, "that Teddington embraces intellectual plurality. We appreciate that Mr. Pedrosian's position is somewhat controversial, but we're rather fond of him, if I may say so. He has been a regular visitor to our campus for several years now, and is the kind of hands-on person we like to bring our girls into contact with."

There were more assurances of Lydia's talents and popularity, then I thanked the vice-dean for her time. What she had told me between the lines was pretty much what I had expected to hear.

Lydia Kravitz was a handful.

● ● ●

Five minutes later, the phone rang. It was Janice.

"You know," she said, "this is one reason why you were always so difficult to live with."

I asked what I'd done now.

"Nutty things happen when you're around," she said. "I just got a phone call telling me to call *you* to tell *you* to look out *your* window. What kind of bullshit is that? If someone wants you to look out the window, fine, but why the hell call me?"

The same blond girl was standing in the park, in the same spot I had seen her before. Lydia? I still couldn't be sure, but it certainly seemed probable. She was looking up at my window, but the moment she was sure I had seen her, she turned and walked slowly away. This time, though, I saw something else. As she drew alongside the pavilion that faces onto 17th Street, she passed very close to a guy with long hair. Maybe she said something to him, or maybe he just took note of her departure, because as soon as she had passed, he looked up at my window.

This time, I didn't rush out, but instead let it go for a while, unobtrusively checking from time to time to make sure the guy was still there. After about half an hour, I went downstairs and left the building, crossed to the park, and walked toward the pavilion. I saw now that it was the hippie kid I had first seen at the Mafioso bar, arguing with Marty Wolfe—the same kid who had sat opposite me, with his girlfriends, when I took a subway downtown after being at the newspaper room. He was pretending to read *Rolling Stone*. I half-expected him to take off when he saw me, but he didn't budge. I paid him no attention and kept going toward the southeast corner of the square. I stopped outside S. Klein, to light a cigarette and to check out if he was following me. He was still pretending to read the magazine, but now he was doing it outside the Union Square Savings Bank. I led him toward the grunge of the Lower East Side, went a couple of blocks south on 2nd Avenue then turned east, headed for Avenue A. When I got there, I rounded the corner and ducked behind a parked truck. As the kid pulled alongside, cursing himself for losing me, I stepped out, grabbed his denim jacket with both hands, put a knee in his groin, and butted him hard in the face with my head. I felt blood spurt from his nose and he went down on his knees, squealing in pain and holding his hands to his face. A semiautomatic—one of those little Rugers—had spilled out onto the sidewalk. I scooped it up and put it in my pocket. I could see there was a wallet in the back pocket of his jeans, so I grabbed that and ran.

Just another Tompkins Square mugging.

●　●　●

It wasn't easy to find a taxi on the Lower East Side in those days, but I got lucky and rode back to my office. By now, I suspected, someone else was probably watching the building, but that was too bad.

I went through the wallet and discovered that it contained drivers' licenses from three different states—New Jersey, Pennsylvania, and California—in three different names. There was also a selection of credit cards to match those licenses, and almost three hundred bucks in mixed bills—a lot of cash for a hippie to be carrying, unless he was dealing. There was a plastic sleeve containing snapshots taken at antiwar demonstrations and some kind of an SDS event. His two girlfriends were in a couple of these photos, but no Lydia, and no Pedrosian. There was a folded scrap of paper with what appeared to be some kind of code or shorthand scrawled on it, and a card, the size of a business card, to which the number 1151 had been applied in red with a rubber stamp. I knew what that was, and kept it aside for later use.

Next, I checked the pistol. It had a full clip and a round in the breech. I opened the safe and was about to put it in with its twin, then changed my mind and instead took out the ankle holster that had been in the Bloomingdale's bag, strapped it to my leg, slipped the hippie's gun into place, and adjusted my Wranglers. It felt strange. I hadn't been fully dressed in a couple of years.

Next I paid a call on Olga. Today she was wearing white running shorts and an orange T-shirt cut off just below the breasts, displaying abs Lionel Hampton could have used for a set of vibes.

I asked her where she got her tan, and she told me I was free to use her sunlamp anytime. I said that what I needed to do right then was to borrow her window. Olga was not the type to ask dumb questions, and invited me to go right ahead. Nothing out there in the park seemed immediately suspicious.

Before I left, Olga mentioned, "Your friend Detective Campbell stopped by earlier."

I asked if he'd inquired after me.

"Your name came up," she said. "I asked him in for a spot of petrissage—told him he'd find it relaxing. He said he wasn't permitted to relax while on duty, but he stuck around a while to look. He seemed especially interested in my shorts, or maybe he just didn't want to look me in the eye. Anyway, there was some small talk of the kind that happens when someone is looking for an excuse to keep on looking, and your name came up. That was about it."

I thanked her and returned to my office. The phone was ringing as I came through the door. It was Mrs. Kravitz. She told me she was worried. She hadn't heard from her husband in more that twenty-four hours, and nobody at his New York office or his Cleveland office had any idea where he was.

I asked if he had a girlfriend. Mrs. Kravitz was predictably annoyed by the question.

"None of your business," she said.

"You told me," I reminded her, "that after you won the beauty contest you began to meet people with interesting tastes. Was Gabe one of them?"

"I don't see what that's got to do with the present situation."

"Let's not be silly. I think you do."

There was a silence at the other end of the line, then she said, "Well, if you must know, Gabe does have a side that you might call kinky. I was able to keep him happy for a long time, but then—well, let's say I grew out of it. I don't know if he did. Probably not, but I imagine that if he gets the itch once in a while, he pays for someone's services. There are places you can go for that sort of thing."

"What sort of thing would that be?"

"C'mon," she said. "Enough's enough. I didn't have to tell you that much and it doesn't have any bearing. With Lydia missing, he's not going to be whoring around."

"So, do you still want me to call off the case?"

"Of course not. I was concerned that getting an investigator involved was stirring things up and making them worse. Now I'm beginning to think it's time to call in the police."

I told her not just yet.

"Why not? This is getting to be a big deal. My husband's a very wealthy man. He could be subject to all kinds of extortion attempts. Kidnapping, blackmail…"

"And who would blackmail him?"

She said nothing.

"Someone familiar with his interesting tastes?" I asked.

"Listen," she said, "I don't even know if he's into anything anymore."

"But if he is, I can think of some situations that would be embarrassing all around."

She thought about that.

"Okay, maybe it's too soon to go to the police," she said, "but I don't know how much longer I can let this go. You don't seem to be getting anywhere."

"Investigations seldom travel in a straight line," I said, "and there's no point in encouraging exaggerated expectations before they're justified."

"Whatever that means," she said. "Sounds like double-talk bullshit to me."

Mrs. Kravitz was not a stupid woman. I told her to try to take it easy, and to let me know the moment she heard anything. I would do likewise.

She had barely hung up when the phone rang again. It was Andrea, and she was just one whiff short of hysterical.

"Someone tried to kill me!" she said.

"Calm down. What happened?"

"*Calm* down? Someone tried to run me over!"

"What were you doing out on the street?" I asked.

"My mother asked me to go to Gristedes to pick up some groceries. I could hardly refuse without making her suspicious. I headed up toward Broadway, and I was crossing the street when suddenly this car came straight at me."

"Are you sure it wasn't an accident?"

"It had pulled out from a parking space, and it came right at me—fast. I don't know how it missed me. Either I just jumped out of the way in time, or he swerved away at the last moment— but he wanted to kill me, or at least to scare the shit out of me."

"The driver was definitely a man?"

"I think so."

"Jerry Pedrosian?"

"I didn't get a good look at him. It all happened in a flash."

"What kind of car?"

"Big old American car. Bright red."

I wanted to believe her story, though I had to admit to a shadow of doubt. The bright red car, though. If this was a story someone had fed her, would they include that detail, since it matched Pedrosian's car? I decided I had to trust her.

"Where are you now?" I asked.

"The subway station at 72nd and Broadway."

"Okay, take a train to Columbus Circle. Walk west on 58th Street and you'll come to an entrance to the Henry Hudson Hotel. Wait for me there, near the desk. If anyone bothers you, tell them you're waiting for your big brother, and clam up."

"What should I do about my parents?"

"Let them stew for a while. It'll be character-building for your mother. Maybe give her some ideas for her next book."

"And what about clothes?" she asked. "Am I supposed to spend the rest of my life in this stupid Lord & Taylor shirtwaist thing?"

I nearly blew my stack at that. Here was a girl with a distorted sense of priorities. Then I found myself softening. I wanted to trust Andrea, and, on reflection, that outburst had helped me to do just that. After all, a preoccupation with clothes, however misguided, was not likely to be prominent in the thoughts of someone who was bent on helping to set up my downfall. That, at least, was what I told myself.

I asked if there was any way I could get into her apartment. She told me she would ring the doorman and tell him to let me in.

● ◌ ●

Fifteen minutes later, I was in Andrea's apartment, or rather her great-aunt's. It was small but comfortable, with minimal furniture. The bedroom contained a double bed and a chest of drawers, and there was a walk-in closet. On a bedside table were two framed photographs of Andrea and Lydia together. In one, they were about fourteen or fifteen, posing on the beach in the kind of bikinis only teenagers have the right to wear. The other had been taken at their high school graduation. In addition, there was a formal portrait of Lydia, backlit and moody.

The living room contained a small dining table, some straight-backed chairs, and a Corbusier recliner, as well as a bookcase filled with volumes that ranged from Beckett to "P. G." Wodehouse. There was a kitchenette, provided with the bare minimum of pots and pans, and a file of take-out menus, plus a tiny bathroom with a shower stall. It was the kind of apartment that all great-aunts should have available to them when they visit New York.

I took five minutes to look around for anything that might have bearing on the case. In the walk-in closet I found what I immediately realized must be Lydia's overnight bag, the one in which Andrea had found the gun. It was dark blue, with a zipper. At first glance, it contained nothing of great interest—a pair of sneakers, some clothing, a couple of schoolbooks, current copies of *Vogue* and *Harper's*. One of the books was a paperback of *The Catcher in the Rye*, and as I picked it up, a folded sheet of paper fell out. On it was a map or diagram of some kind, crudely sketched and accompanied by a key written in the same code or shorthand that I had found on the scrap of paper in the hippie's wallet.

I put it in my pocket and began to pick out some clothes for Andrea, enjoying the task a little more than I should have. I packed my choices in a small suitcase and headed uptown, deliberately taking an indirect route that included the Port Authority Bus Terminal—a good place to shake anybody who might be following—a further detour through Peek-a-Boo Books on 42nd Street, then a taxi to the Park Central Hotel, where I exited by the rear entrance before finishing my journey to the Henry Hudson on foot.

● ● ●

The Henry Hudson Hotel began life as a residence for young women, since then it has gone through a number of transformations. In 1968, it had a mixed clientele that included a sizable number of African Americans, many with showbiz aspirations, and gay men of all races, including members of the Warhol crowd. I figured it was not the first place anyone would think of to look for me and Andrea. She seemed relieved to see me. I checked us in, asking for a room with two beds, which caused the clerk to raise an eyebrow.

"Do you think Mom will call tonight?" Andrea threw in casually. "Does she know we're in town yet?"

The girl was catching on.

Our room was near the top of the building, with a window that overlooked 57th Street near the intersection with Broadway. It was hardly luxurious—funky even—but clean, there was a TV, and it was big enough to hole up in for a while without going stir crazy.

"Where do I sleep?" Andrea asked.

"I'll take the bed closest to the door," I said.

Andrea looked at me quizzically.

"Is that to stop me making a run for it," she asked, "or to be ready when somebody bursts in with a gun in their hand?"

"A bit of both," I told her.

She began to unpack the clothes I had brought for her, laying them out on the bed.

"I guess you do think I'm sexy." She giggled.

I liked that giggle more every time I heard it. She asked me to turn my back. When she said it was okay to turn around again, she was dressed in a denim miniskirt and a T-shirt—pretty much the outfit she had had on that first evening.

"Was that true," I asked, "that you've only slept with one guy?"

I should have left that alone, but my curiosity had gotten the better of me.

She just smiled and said she was hungry, so we looked at the room service menu and ordered a couple of sandwiches and some beer. While we were waiting, I told her what had happened since I had left her in the coffee shop. There didn't seem to be any sense in hiding it from her, whichever side she was on. She liked the part about me ambushing the hippie.

"You actually mugged the guy? You kneed him in the balls and you mugged him?"

She was impressed.

"You *are* useful to have around," she said.

I showed her the scrap of paper, with the scribbled code, that I'd taken from the hippie, and the schematic map that I'd found inside Lydia's copy of *The Catcher in the Rye*.

"She must have read that book a hundred times," said Andrea. "She says she reads it when she gets down on herself."

"But what about this writing?" I asked. "Seems to be some kind of code. Does it mean anything to you?"

"You bet your ass," said Andrea. "That's Lydia's writing. You may find this hard to believe, but her mother began life as a typist-stenographer. I've told you how smart Lydia is. She's one of those people who can pick up languages and stuff just like that— French, Italian. She went to Sweden one summer and came back talking fluent Swedish. A few years ago, she figured out that she could do her homework much quicker if she learned shorthand, so she got her mother to teach her."

"Can you read it?"

"Are you kidding? Not me! But Lydia's a wiz."

Something occurred to her, and her expression changed.

"Does this mean she's in real trouble? I mean, you took that paper from the hippie who was following you with a gun in his pants."

Just then there was a knock on the door and I let the room service waiter in. He set us up, I tipped him, and he left.

"It means," I said, "that's she's gotten herself mixed up with something potentially dangerous, but I still don't know what."

I showed her the card with the rubber-stamped number on it.

"Do you know what that is?" I said.

"I know Lydia has one. She told me it's a membership card for some kind of a club."

"A place called the Tea Bag," I said. "A very private club with music and a lot of potheads. That's why they call it the Tea Bag."

We ate our sandwiches, and as I finished my beer, I saw that Andrea was staring at my right ankle. Seated at the room service trolley, I had let the cuffs of my jeans ride up, revealing the automatic in its holster.

"Now *you're* wearing a gun," she said. "That means that this is all real. That car really did try to kill me!"

"Or at least scare you."

"Yeah, well it did that, but I was just beginning to kid myself that I'd been jaywalking or daydreaming or something. But you don't believe that, do you?"

"Jerry Pedrosian has a red car, an old Pontiac."

"Jesus! So we're not here in this hotel room for a cozy chat about the weather."

"And now," I said, "I've got to go out for a while, so be good and don't leave this room under any circumstances."

She looked panicked.

"Where are you going?"

"I'm following up on a couple of leads."

"What kind of leads?"

"I'll tell you later."

"Can't I come with you?"

I told her no, and to avoid prolonging the scene I made for the door. She blocked my way, looked up into my eyes, and hugged me. As hugs go, this one got two thumbs up.

"Promise me," she said, "that you'll be careful."

● ● ●

So why was it that I still didn't completely trust the lovely Andrea? Maybe because I didn't trust myself *with* the lovely Andrea, so I found it convenient to impute all kinds of sordid intentions to her. Or maybe because I couldn't totally eradicate from my head the image of her picking up the house phone the moment I was out the door and calling Lydia or Pedrosian to check on her orders for the next few hours. For a moment, that image was so strong that I slipped the key back into the lock and silently opened the door. Andrea was on her bed, quietly crying. She sat up, with a look of pure happiness on her face.

"You changed your mind?"

"No," I said, "I've got to go, but I wanted to say, make sure the door is locked and on the chain at all times."

FOURTEEN

So I rode down in the elevator, feeling like a heel. I hung around the lobby for a while, to make sure that no one suspicious was getting his shoes shined, then walked to the Columbus Circle subway station and took a train down to the Village. The entrance to the Tea Bag was an anonymous-looking door next to a shoe store on 8th Street. To get in to the joint you had to go through the old Prohibition routine of knocking on the door and waiting for someone to check you out through a spy hole. I knocked and a voice from behind the door said, "Are you sure you've got the right place, brother?"

I held up the hippie's card and said, "I'm here to see Otis."

The guy behind the door still didn't seem sure, but he let me in. He was a big black guy in shades, a black T-shirt, black pants, black sneakers, and one brown glove.

"You sure you know Otis?" he said.

"Otis and I go way back," I said.

That was true. I first met Otis in the holding cell when I was busted. We'd stayed in touch. I'd heard he was managing the Tea Bag, but hadn't been there to see him till now. The bouncer directed me down a narrow flight of stairs, toward a lot of noise of the Stax variety, and a nimbus of aromatic smoke. At the bottom was a window with a reinforced glass panel that could be slid open. As I approached, the panel opened, a hand with a pink palm emerged, and we slapped some skin. Otis invited me into his office, offered me the choice between a joint the size of a baby's forearm and a firkin of vodka, and asked why I hadn't been around to see him before.

"I'm getting too old for these scenes," I said. "Next birthday's the big three-oh. Five years from now I won't be able to trust myself."

"I don't trust myself now," said Otis. "You should lay eyes on some of the good bait out there, man. And they'll do anything you want for a nickel bag."

We chatted for a couple of minutes and Otis said, "So you're not here to buy, you're not here to dance, and you're not here to get laid. You must be working."

I took out the rubber-stamped card and asked if there was any way of identifying who it had been issued to.

Otis shrugged.

"We just hand 'em out, man. A place like this, you don't keep records."

I showed him the snapshots of Lydia.

"Ever see this chick?"

He looked at the pictures, smiled, and nodded.

"Friend of yours?" he asked.

"I never met her."

"Yeah, she's been in here," he said. "You don't miss that chick. Comes in with an older guy who likes to hang out with cute young ass."

"Who doesn't," I said, not without a pang of guilt. "What does this guy look like?"

"Reminds me some of that Steve McQueen dude. Thinks he's hot shit."

That sounded like Pedrosian.

"He comes here with other girls?"

"Yeah, but he's been with this blond bitch the last few times. Man, she's a wild one, and dishes out plenty sass. They were here last Friday or Saturday, and I had to have Mohommad throw them out. There were a couple of boys here in uniform that night. Fact is, they didn't really belong here, but they told me they were off to 'Nam in a couple of days, and I thought why the fuck not let them have a good time if they're going to get their ass napalmed before their next birthday. Your blond bitch here, and her dude, and a couple of other kids, really got on 'em—called them pigs, murderers, the whole sick-assed fuck the flag bit. And she was the worst, screaming her fuckin' lungs out, man! They were flying on some heavy shit."

● ● ●

When I got out of there, I called Andrea from an ice cream parlor on 6th. She said she was fine, and was watching *The Flying Nun*. Next I headed for 14th Street. In those days, you could get almost anything on 14th Street except a good latte. Since I walked to my office that way almost every day, I was familiar with most all of the businesses that had storefronts or signs visible from the street. Samantha Smart's 24-Hour Secretarial School was above a discount cosmetics store between 6th and 7th Avenues, near the Salvation Army. Its sign featured a painting of a young woman with a Veronica Lake hairdo, ample boobs, and killer legs, poised in front of a typewriter that looked as if it might have been jiggered together by Dr. Frankenstein. The artist had evidently spent a great deal of time thinking about girls, but not much looking at typewriters.

I rang the doorbell and a voice with a Brooklyn accent crackled out of a small speaker attached to the doorframe. I saw that I was being spied on by a closed-circuit television camera.

"What can I do for you, darling?" the voice asked.

I told it I had some questions about shorthand.

"We can teach you Pitman in three weeks, six hours a day, or six weeks, three hours a day," said the voice.

"Unfortunately, I don't have time for that," I said.

"Then I can't help you," said the voice, "unless you want to take our crash course in turning paper clips into costume jewelry."

I showed the closed circuit camera my license.

"I don't have my reading glasses," said the voice, disinterested.

"I'm a detective," I said, trying to be helpful.

"A detective?" yawned the voice. "How very exciting. I never thought in my whole life I'd ever get to meet another real live detective. On 14th Street, yet."

She buzzed me in and I walked up a flight of stairs to find a bleached blonde, in the early stages of finding out that it was too late. She was wrapped in a pink, hand-knitted jacket and peering at me through jeweled harlequin glasses. She sat behind a Formica desk with a white Princess phone, an open book, and a vase of artificial tulips.

I asked if she was Samantha Smart. She said she was Darleen, dumb enough to be working the graveyard shift. Samantha Smart, God bless her, had joined the great typing pool in the sky. I told her I'd heard they were retraining people up there to carve stone tablets. She said, "That's right, make fun of my religion."

I showed her the pieces of paper with Lydia's shorthand on them.

"Sloppy," she said, "but confident. You can tell a lot about someone from their shorthand, just like you can from their handwriting. This is someone in a big hurry to make their mark. Look at those loops. Very assertive. I like the calligraphy. Shows an impetuous temperament."

"But what does it say?" I prompted.

She studied the diagram first.

"There's not much to go by here. There are words like *high window* and *escape route*. Is this something about a prison break or something? This down here says *clock tower*, and these signs on the right stand for *upper house* and *lower house*. That's about all I can tell you about that one."

Upper house and lower house? Something to do with Congress? Or some state legislature? That seemed ominous.

Darleen looked at the other scrap of paper and screwed up her face.

"This one's even worse," she said. "There's something about putty, and this word is *aromatic*. But then there are words that don't mean anything to me—*semtex, cyclonite*. Seems kind of scientific."

I made notes and thanked her. She returned to her novel. The title was *The Lady and the Scoundrel*. The author was Alyson Marshall.

● ● ●

From the street, I called Janice to ask her to feed Samba. She wasn't happy about that. I told her I'd take her to see *Rosencrantz and Guildenstern*.

As I left the booth, I saw someone staring at me. Another skinny kid with long hair. He wasn't even pretending to be invisible. That pissed me off. I walked over to him and said, "This is getting on my fucking nerves."

He told me to fuck off, and bunched his fists as if he was going to hit me, which wasn't a smart thing to do. I grabbed his wrist and twisted his arm behind his back, jerking it hard so that it hurt.

"Bastard!" he said, which I thought was pretty polite under the circumstances.

"Why don't you go back to Pedrosian," I said, "and tell him to go fuck himself?"

This didn't seem to register.

"Huh?" was all he said.

"I'm fed up of being followed everywhere," I said.

"I wasn't following you," he said.

"Then why were you staring at me?"

"Because I recognized you, and it was the second time tonight I'd seen you."

Now I was confused.

"I saw you come out of Andrea's building," he said, "carrying a suitcase."

Now the penny dropped.

"Is your name Jonathon?"

He said it was and I let him go.

"Bastard," he said again. "People like you should be shot. She's too good for you and you're old enough to be her father."

That hurt.

"You want to get technical," I said, "I'm old enough to be her big brother."

"Fuck you," he said. "What have you done with her?"

"First, you tell me why you were spying on Andrea's building."

"I wasn't. I just went there to see if she was home. Then I saw you come out of the building with a suitcase."

He spat in the gutter.

"We need to get something straight," I told him. "First of all, there's nothing going on between me and Andrea. I haven't touched her."

Saying that reminded me of that two-thumbs-up hug.

"Why should I believe that?" the boy said.

"Because I say so."

"So where is she? I want to see her."

"You're going to take this the wrong way, but I can't tell you." The boy sneered.

"What did Andrea tell you about me?" I asked.

"That you're some kind of a detective, something to do with that slut Lydia. Not that I really bought that shit."

"You know Lydia?"

"Not really, but I know she's a slut. Andrea gets excited when she talks about her. It's like Lydia's slutty affairs turn her on. I hate it."

"You remember that bag Andrea was carrying the other night, when you were keeping an eye on us? Do you know what was in it?"

"How would I know? It was none of my business. She'd told me that meeting you had something to do with buying dope. I offered to go for her. She wouldn't let me, but she said I could keep an eye on things. I wasn't happy about any of it, especially when the two of you went into the restaurant. She hadn't told me about anything like that, and she didn't tell me about the detective business until we were back in my room. I thought she was making it up, but, hey, I wanted to believe her story because it was Andrea."

I could dig that feeling, and I figured he was being straight with me. A little wet behind the ears, maybe, but that wasn't a crime.

"Let's go somewhere quiet and talk," I suggested.

● ◦ ●

He was a pleasant-looking kid with freckles and a lot of teeth. Norman Rockwell would have liked him, or painted him anyway. I took him to a Cuban-Chinese place that was almost empty, and ordered coffees. I told him that Andrea might be in danger, but that I couldn't tell him why. He swallowed that more readily than I'd expected.

"I'd like to help," he said, in a gee-whiz voice that made me expect the next words out of his mouth to be something like "Holy hockey sticks, Batman!"

I wanted to tell him to just stay the hell out of the way, but thought it would be smarter to hold out a prospect of participation, however illusory.

"There's nothing you can do at the moment," I told him. "I'd like to keep you on hold for now, so that no one suspects your involvement. I may need your help later. I presume Andrea knows how to reach you?"

"Of course. I've got a room on Cornelia Street. "

My meaningless gesture seemed to have cleansed him of all suspicion about my intentions, and now he eagerly quizzed me about Andrea, and her feelings for him.

"She talked about you quite a bit," I told him. "I don't like to pry, but I got the impression you were her boyfriend. That was about it. I didn't ask if you were good in bed."

I meant that as a joke, but I could tell from Jonny's expression that it didn't go down that way. He was embarrassed to the point of being humiliated.

"I didn't sleep with her yet," he said, as if admitting to extreme dereliction of duty.

I apologized for speaking out of turn and, after a while, I got up to leave. I told Jonny to finish his coffee and wait at least ten minutes before he left the restaurant.

He nodded solemnly, as if to say, "You can count on me, chief."

● ● ●

I headed uptown by another circuitous route that included a detour through an automat in the garment district, and another through the Hotel Pennsylvania, which was crowded with uniformed flight crew fresh in from JFK and LaGuardia. When I got back to the Henry Hudson, I called Andrea from the house phone in the lobby, and told her I was on my way up, but not to open the door till I got there. She answered my knock wearing a T-shirt and a pair of underpants.

"You didn't bring anything for me to sleep in," she said, apologetically.

There was no hug, this time, and she said she was beat. I gave her a quick rundown of my conversation with Otis at the Tea Bag, but decided not to mention anything about my visit to the secretarial school for the moment. I did, though, give an account of my encounter with Jonathon, telling her pretty much everything, but leaving out the bit about him admitting he hadn't fucked her.

"Poor Jonny," she said. "He's a nice boy, but confused. He grew up somewhere near Indianapolis and went to a boys' school that sounds like it was almost like a military academy. When he arrived here, he had short hair, like a soldier. I introduced him to Lydia back then, and she made some nasty remarks about him having a grunt cut. That's one reason he doesn't like her. But he's been growing his hair ever since, and it looks cute, didn't you think? Unfortunately, growing your hair is the easy bit. The rest doesn't come that easily."

"But why did you tell him you were meeting with me to buy dope that night?"

"Come on! Didn't you ever hear of a cover story? You of all people. I didn't want him to know it was something to do with

Lydia. I did tell him afterward, but anything to do with Lydia gets him pissed."

"He said he thought Lydia's exploits turned you on?"

Andrea was angry.

"That's because he's a prude."

"So do you tease him with Lydia's sexual exploits?"

"What? You know, you ask too many questions. I don't want to get into any of that now. I'm beat. I'm going to sleep."

She climbed into bed and turned out the bedside lamp. I removed the ankle holster—glad to be free of it—turned out the rest of the lights, and lay down on the other bed, fully clothed. An hour later, I could tell from her breathing that Andrea was still awake. Across the gap between the two beds, I could smell the same fragrance that had clung to the sheets in my apartment after she was there, a fragrance that can't be bought off the shelf. It was intoxicating and I needed to get away from it before it got me drunk. It also made me think of something else—the word aromatic. It was a word that Darleen at the secretarial school had decoded for me. I checked the time. 1:35. Just 10:35 in California. In a whisper, I asked Andrea if she was still awake. She said yes in a way that could have been taken, by a suitably deranged person, as anticipatory. I told her I was going downstairs for a few minutes, that I had something to check out.

She said, "Hurry back."

I put my shoes on and went down to the lobby, which was still busy, found a phone booth, and placed a call to my childhood pal Bernie Kupchik, who was now a research chemist at the University of California, Berkeley. As I thumbed through my notebook, we exchanged pleasantries, then I said, "Okay, I've got a couple of words for you."

He said, "Shoot."

"The first is semtex."

"That's interesting," he said. "And the next?"

"The next is cyclonite."

"Well, that's pretty interesting, and I'll tell you for free those are not the names of patent sleep remedies. Semtex is a kind of plastic explosive. It's manufactured in Czechoslovakia and I hear it's popular with the Viet Cong for blowing up just about anything you can stick it to. The stuff is like putty. I don't know if Semtex is available on this side of the Atlantic, but if it is, it would be popular here, too, for uses like commercial blasting and demolition work. Cyclonite, usually called RDX, is the actual explosive component in several different plastic explosives. It's been around quite a while and is found in something called C4—Composition 4—which is a very common form of plastique. Our boys in Vietnam like C4 for a bunch of reasons. For example, if you borrow a bit from a Claymore mine—about the size of an M&M will do—and swallow it, it'll make you very sick and with a bit of luck you'll be pulled off the front line. C4 is also very common in the US for blasting and demolition gigs."

"Anything aromatic about this stuff?"

"Well, it isn't Chanel Number Five, but nitrated aromatics are used in manufacturing putty explosives, which is what the pros call them."

This was pretty heavy. I thanked Bernie and headed back upstairs. Andrea was waiting for me.

"Everything okay?" she asked.

"Anything but," I said.

"Are you going to tell me?"

"I'll tell you in the morning. It's going to be a big day, so get some sleep."

I turned the lights off again, then had a thought.

"I know Lydia's father is in the construction business, but does he have anything to do with demolition?"

"Oh, sure," said Andrea. "Once Lydia and I went out to Coney Island to see a big old hotel knocked down. You know—just one little puff of smoke and the whole thing comes down in slow motion. It was on television, on the news. That was her dad's company that did that. They do it all over America—in other countries, too."

This was getting heavier by the minute.

FIFTEEN

There were days when I felt like I was playing at being a detective. It was fun, and I was pretty good at it—a utility infielder who hit for a decent average—but it was still just a game, and even though my work sometimes involved paintings worth millions of dollars, it was only pretend money, like the bills used to buy Marvin Gardens or a railroad company on the Monopoly board.

This was not one of those days.

I told Andrea everything that I knew. There didn't seem to be any point in holding back anything at that stage of the game.

"Plastic explosives," she said. "Those are dangerous, aren't they?"

"If you don't know what you're doing with them."

"And how would someone like Lydia know what she was doing?"

"You said her father has a company that does demolition work. Could that have given her the opportunity to learn something about explosives?"

Andrea shrugged.

I told her about my interrupted visit to the house on Ladies Lane.

"I only saw firearms, but who knows what might have been on the other floors—explosives, fuses, timing devices. It could have been a whole bomb factory."

"Is that down near Canal?" Andrea asked. "I met Lydia somewhere near Canal when she was here about a month ago. We were going to Chinatown."

"That place was probably their safe house."

"Okay, but what would they want to blow up?"

"Who knows? Chances are it's something to do with the war. They might want to hit a draft board office, or some military installation—anything to do with the military. Or maybe they just want to do something symbolic, like blow up a statue. There's a few of those I'd like to blow up. I don't know. Could be they're just playing dangerous games, but I'm beginning to get the picture that Jerry Pedrosian is into some pretty heavy stuff. He's always had a nose for the latest fad, and his career hasn't been going too well, so he has time on his hands for mischief. What about Lydia?"

"Lydia likes to be provocative, whether she's talking about sex or socialism. She always takes the contrary position. At school, she was the first one against the war. That's just the way she is."

"Yeah, I'm against the war, too, but in Lydia's case it seems to have led her into some pretty scary territory."

Andrea nodded.

"I guess that's what I was afraid of," she said.

I showed her the map.

"Do you know of anywhere that has a bell tower, an upper house and a lower house?"

"Well, yes," said Andrea. "I know of at least two places. One is the Palace of Westminster—the British Houses of Parliament to you. Big Ben is in the clock tower, and the parliament consists of the House of Lords and the House of Commons. The other place is Crufts."

"Crufts? The school that you and Lydia went to?"

"That's right. Dr. Grimsby, the founder, was a big admirer of the British parliamentary system. He insisted on the school building having a clock tower, which is named—you guessed it—Little Ben. As the school got bigger, it expanded into the building next door. The original building houses the older kids, the other one the younger kids—the Upper House, and the Lower House. Apparently, that was Dr. Grimsby's idea of humor. But if you're thinking that Lydia would want to blow up Crufts, there's no way. She had plenty of problems while she was there, but basically she had a great time. I mean, we were the in crowd."

I agreed that the school seemed to be an unlikely target.

"So where do we go from here?" Andrea asked.

"I don't know. It's reached the point where probably I should pick up that phone and call the police."

"No!" said Andrea, fiercely.

"Why not?"

"Because, if the police are involved, what are they going to do to Lydia?"

"If Lydia's involved in something that is endangering people's lives, the police will do what they have to do."

I didn't mention that I had my own reasons for being reluctant to call the police, since they would have plenty of questions about why I hadn't come to them earlier. A missing persons investigation is one thing. Not reporting a cache of weapons is something else.

"She's still my friend. I don't want her to be shot or something."

"Let me remind you," I said, "that someone tried to run you down and maybe kill you yesterday afternoon. Not a friendly act."

"She didn't know about it."

"How can you be sure of that?"

"Because I know her, that's how. If Jerry Pedrosian, or someone else, tried to run me down yesterday it happened without Lydia knowing anything about it."

I tried to convince myself she was right. There had been those visits by the blond girl to my apartment, and my office building. What were those about? And there had been that telephone call that led me to the building on Ladies Lane. That had sounded like a cry for help, but it could equally have been setting me up.

"We've been friends for twelve years," said Andrea. "I can practically read Lydia's mind."

"Well, get started," I said. "We could use a bit of psychic help."

She was angry and so was I, and some of my doubts about her were returning. She stormed into the bathroom, and I heard the shower running.

I switched on the television and found a local news show. A gaggle of pundits was gabbing about Bobby Kennedy's chances in the upcoming California primary when there was a newsflash. Reports were coming in of an explosion in a townhouse near Gramercy Park. Early footage showed that the top two floors of the building had been completely demolished. Several neighbors said they had seen people running from the building. There was disagreement as to the numbers, but at least two men and a woman had been spotted. Another told the on-scene reporter that the property had been empty since it was sold several months earlier, and was scheduled to undergo a major renovation. The present owner, he added, was rumored to be the wife of City Councilman Donald Baldridge.

I turned from the television to see Andrea standing in the doorway to the bathroom, wrapped in a towel, her hand held over her mouth, her eyes wide.

"Oh, my God!" she said.

A fire department spokesman was saying that the cause was unclear at that point, and that the department would be looking into all possibilities.

"Poor Lydia," said Andrea.

I told her that this was no time for "poor Lydia."

"Do you think she got away?" she asked.

I asked her what made her so sure that Lydia had been there. I did not recall mentioning Baldridge's name when I told her about the Ladies Lane building, nor had I had any reason to tell her that Pedrosian was Baldridge's brother-in-law.

"What makes you think she was there?" I said. "Are you holding out on me?"

Andrea was startled by my question.

"The house blew up," she said. "Houses don't just blow up by themselves. It must have been a bomb, and we know who has been playing with bombs, don't we?"

"It could have been a gas explosion," I said.

"It could have been, but you don't believe that, do you?"

"I'm in no position to guess."

"Three people seen running from the building," said Andrea. "Two men and a young woman…"

"In any case," I said, "now we *have* to go to the police. You'd better get some clothes on. I'll be in the bathroom."

I stepped into the bathroom and just seconds later I heard the door to the room slam. If I had run after her, I might have caught her, but if she had an ounce of sense in her head—and by now I was beginning to believe she did—she would have screamed bloody murder. Getting caught with a naked eighteen-year-old in a hotel corridor wasn't going to help anybody.

I can't exactly explain why, but I experienced an enormous sense of relief. The last vestige of game playing was over. It was time to get serious.

● ● ●

Then I saw that Andrea had taken the gun and the holster. I had left them in full view on a chair. That had been pretty dumb of me. I opened the door and looked out into the corridor. A room service waiter was telling a chambermaid that he'd just seen a girl—stark naked and clutching a bundle of clothes—headed for the emergency stairs. They turned to look at me, and the waiter grinned.

If Andrea was getting dressed on the stairs, which was likely, I might still catch her, but there was no point. I didn't trust her, and that changed everything.

There was no point hanging around. Andrea had already drawn attention to herself, so it would be a matter of minutes, and not many of those, before the house detective paid a visit. I went back into the room, put on my shoes and grabbed my wallet, then headed downstairs and out into the street, just in time to see Andrea—more or less dressed—jump into a taxi that headed west on 57th Street. Did she have some idea of where she might find Lydia, or Pedrosian? No way of knowing.

I ducked into the lobby of an office building and found a booth with a set of phone books. I looked up the address of Crufts Academy for Young Ladies. It was just half a dozen blocks from the townhouse where the explosion had occurred. That was interesting. I took a taxi downtown toward Gramercy Park, but before I got that far, I could see that the streets up ahead were clogged with police vehicles, fire trucks, ambulances, and television news vans. So I got out and covered the last stretch to the school on foot. I spotted it as I turned east off 3rd Avenue—a vaguely Gothic structure with a clock tower that bore a remote resemblance to its sibling in the City of Westminster.

Things were quiet around there, except for the shouts and yells of a group of girls in plaid school uniforms playing volleyball beyond a chain-link fence. My quest was to find something nearby that might be singled out as a target by a group of fringe radical hotheads with a supply of guns and explosives. I didn't have to look far. Directly across the street from the school was an elegant Greek Revival townhouse, with fancy ironwork and dark green marble columns. Attached to the railings outside was a brass plate that identified the building as the headquarters of the Barnes Institute for Military Strategy, a think tank notorious for the virulence of its anti-Communist dogma and its supposed influence inside the Pentagon. In particular, BIMS had become identified with promoting the search-and-destroy tactics that had seen American and South Vietnamese ground troops and air cavalry engaged in a brutal war of attrition against the Viet Cong. These tactics were responsible for untold numbers of civilians being killed, maimed, or dispossessed of their homes and livelihoods.

I could empathize with radicals who looked at this handsome Victorian edifice and contemplated the contrast with the burning bamboo huts in Binh Duong Province. That didn't stop me from making an anonymous call to 911 from a callbox on the street, which was quickly forwarded to someone at Police Headquarters who was more interested in knowing my name than in what I had to pass along. I kept my name to myself and delivered my information as succinctly as possible. He finally got the picture.

I reported that the explosion near Gramercy Park had been caused by a bomb. I told him that the headquarters of the Barnes Institute for Military Strategy was probably under threat of attack. I recommended that Crufts Academy should be evacuated as a precaution, and I gave him the names that I knew, including Lydia Kravitz. I also mentioned Pedrosian's red Pontiac, and warned that it might contain explosives (though I doubted that anyone would be using such a conspicuous car at this stage of the game). Then I cleaned my prints from the receiver and got out of there, trying not to draw attention to myself as the sirens of patrol cars converged on the area.

I walked to my office, which wasn't that far. I had to presume that it was all too probable that someone—either Pedrosian's mob, or the police, or both—would be watching the building, but there was nothing I could do about that. As I walked, I tried to figure out what would be going through the minds of Pedrosian and Lydia—assuming they were still alive. Andrea, too. What the hell was she up to? Did she know where to find them? Or how to contact them? Or was she on some personal mission? Part of me still refused to believe that she was in league with the crazies.

As I walked through Union Square, I saw a police car parked directly outside my building. Detective Campbell was leaning on it, talking to a couple of uniformed cops inside. After a minute or two, he got into the back of the car and it drove off. I had no reason to suppose that the cops were on to me, except for the fact that Campbell had been hanging around an awful lot lately. I decided to take some elementary precautions. There was a way of getting to the back stairs by going through the kitchen of the Chinese restaurant on the ground floor, and out into the little courtyard where they kept their garbage cans. I reached my office without encountering anyone who spoke English, and let myself in.

There were messages on my Ansaphone. The first was from Janice who said she thought Samba had colic. The second was from Gabriel Kravitz. He apologized for having been out of touch, but said that he had decided to call off the investigation.

"It's 6:35 a.m.," he said. "I suspect that I rather overreacted to the unfortunate situation between Lydia and Mr. Pedrosian. As you pointed out, Lydia is not a minor, and therefore is legally responsible for her own decisions. I have spoken to Mrs. Kravitz about this, and she fully concurs. You will, of course, be properly compensated for your time, and a bonus will be included since I remain concerned that none of this should find its way into the media."

Next came a message from Mrs. Kravitz.

"I wanted to let you know that I've heard from Gabe. It seems he's been in Canada, but he's back in town, and he called me from the airport when he flew in. I think you've probably heard from him by now and have been told that we've decided to call off the search for Lydia—definitively this time. Thank you for your efforts."

These two calls had all the spontaneity of an Academy Awards acceptance speech. Something had happened that had brought the Kravitzes down to earth with a bump. By now, it could be assumed, they'd received another rude shock, thanks to my 911 call. For the hell of it, I called the number that Mrs. Kravitz had given me—her boudoir number. It was answered by a male voice with a generic tristate accent that informed me that Mrs. Kravitz was unable to come to the phone.

"Is that Sergeant Sardotti?" I asked, pulling a name out of the air.

"No. This is Officer Chevinsky."

So the cops were already there. Good to know.

There were a couple more messages, one of them from Mrs. Baldridge.

"For what it's worth," she said, "you were right about Jerry using that building on Ladies Lane. Donald had given him permission, so there was nothing underhanded about it. I don't know quite why you were so interested, but my advice is you might as well drop it, whatever it is. Even if Jerry was schtupping his little bimbo there, it's academic because the building's empty now, and will stay that way. We'll just have to let Jerry get on with his life, won't we?"

A touching display of disinterested sisterly concern. Given what had happened at the Gramercy Park townhouse, I suspected that by now Mrs. Baldridge, like Mrs. Kravitz, would find herself covered in NYPD fuzz.

I turned on the radio to see if I could catch a bulletin updating the explosion. The story was all over the airwaves. The police were refusing to confirm rumors that the explosion had been caused by a bomb, but an unnamed source "close to a federal agency" suggested that it had been the result of an accidental detonation caused by "radical extremists" in the process of manufacturing some kind of an explosive device. A rescue worker had reported seeing what appeared to be body parts. It was reiterated that neighbors had observed people fleeing the house, though a police spokesman warned that these might have been bystanders reacting to the explosion.

I walked to my window, and looked down into the park. She was there, the ethereal blond girl, standing in the spot where she always stood, dressed in jeans and a white shirt. This time, she didn't look away when she saw me.

SIXTEEN

I fetched the other pistol from my wall safe, slipped it in my jacket pocket, then hurried down the stairs and out into the street, not even thinking of the possibility that the cops might be staked out for me.

She was still there, waiting, and now I was close enough to see that it definitely was Lydia. As I crossed the street, she turned and walked away from me, but slowly, not attempting to lose me. My first thought was that she could be leading me into a trap, but it didn't feel like that, and Union Square in broad daylight didn't seem a likely place for an ambush. So I followed, closing to within maybe twenty feet, till she sat down on a bench. I sat down next to her, but left space between us. She didn't look at me, just stared straight ahead. I did the same.

"Where's Andrea?" she asked.

"I was going to ask you the same thing," I told her. "Where's Pedrosian?"

"I don't know. He might be dead, for all I know. I hope so."

"Didn't he get out of the building with you?"

"I wasn't there. All I know is what I saw on TV in a coffee shop."

This was getting more confusing by the minute.

"Whether he's alive or dead," she said, "I'm through with Jerry Pedrosian. There've been too many shocks, and when I found out what he did to Andrea yesterday, that was the end."

"So that was real? He was trying to kill her?"

"Or maim her, or scare her. Just make sure she was out of the picture one way or the other."

I finally looked at her, and she at me, but only for a second.

"Why," I asked, "did he want her out of the picture so badly?"

"Because he thought she knew too much."

"What did she know that was so terrible?"

"You'll find out. In time."

A police cruiser paused, a few feet away, then moved on.

"And don't even think about calling down the cops," said Lydia. "When this is resolved maybe I'll give myself up. But not till then. And don't imagine you can make me do anything I don't want to do."

Her fist was in her bag, and she showed me that it was clutching the butt of a Ruger semiautomatic, just like the one I had in my jacket pocket. It would probably have been easy enough to disarm her, but it was too soon to exercise that option. There was a lot more I needed to know before I showed my hand.

"Now that we understand one another," she said, "let's start again. Where's Andrea?"

"Same answer. I wish I knew. I had her holed up at the Henry Hudson Hotel, if you know where that is. This morning, we found out about the explosion in the townhouse on the TV news. All she could think of was that something bad might have happened to you. The first chance she got, she took off—to find you, I presume—and, for what it's worth, she took my gun."

153

"Great!" said Lydia. "I'm looking for Andrea, and she's look-ing for me, and she's carrying a gun, which she doesn't know one end of from the other. And Pedrosian—if he's alive—is looking for both of us, and he does know how to use a gun. And any-way, what made Andrea think I had anything to do with that townhouse?"

I ignored that last question.

"Who was in the house when it blew?" I asked.

"Like I told you, I wasn't there. When I did my disappear-ing act yesterday, Jerry was there with Homer—that's the kid you bushwhacked—and his two sisters, Lucy and Crystal. At least, he claims they're his sisters. They've dropped so much acid they don't know who they are, but the bottom line is they'll do any-thing Jerry tells them to. Then there was Lanny and Rick, Jerry's ex-army buddies. Have you run into those creeps?"

"I didn't even know Jerry was in the army."

"Oh, yeah. End of World War II—a demolitions expert. When they got out of the service, Lanny, Rick, and Jerry all got GI Bill scholarships, hung out together at the clubs on 52nd Street, and called themselves hipsters. Lanny plays some guitar, and later he got into the Village folk scene—hanging out with Dylan and Dave Van Ronk and the political crowd—and he was in with a bunch of Trotskyites. I don't know Rick's story. Just went along for the ride, I guess, but these guys know a shitload about bombs and that kind of crap. They talk about crafting explosives like it's some kind of folk art, and that's the way Jerry sees things, too. The world needs to be rearranged, he likes to say, and there's nothing like a stick of dynamite to move things around."

"Is that what he was teaching at Teddington?"

"Well, he watered it down a bit for the course, but that's what he told me after he fucked me down by the lake one night."

"So Lanny and Rick were at the house?"

"Maybe yes, maybe no. I have no way of knowing. They came and went. They were in on everything, but they operated in a more freelance way. They share an apartment somewhere in Queens."

"And when did you become disenchanted?" I prompted.

Finally, she looked me in the eye.

"You ask too many questions," she said. "You'll get answers, but only after we've found Andrea."

"What about Pedrosian? What's he going to do next? Was he planning a hit on the Barnes Institute?"

Lydia hadn't expected that.

"How did you know?"

"I figured it out with some help from Andrea."

"Well, now help me figure out where to find her. You can worry about the other stuff later."

"Did you and Andrea have any special places?" I asked. "Places she might go to look for you? When she ran out on me at the hotel, she didn't know if you were alive or dead, but she would assume that if you were alive you were on the run—maybe with Pedrosian, maybe on your own. Is there anywhere you would go to hide out that she might know about?" Lydia thought about that for a moment. She showed me the gun again.

"Let's go," she said. "Don't ask questions and don't get cute. We're just going a couple of blocks."

●　●　●

It may have been just a couple of blocks, but I had plenty to chew on. What had happened between Lydia and Pedrosian? I could understand that she was enraged about the attempted rundown, but I was sure that there was more to the falling out than that. And if she had been looking to me for help before, why didn't she say so? Perhaps she saw her own situation as being beyond help at this point. Now she was solely focused on keeping Andrea out of trouble. These girls were crazy, but their devotion to one another was impressive.

We crossed 14th Street and headed south on University Place. Two blocks later, Lydia said, "Take a right here," and as we turned west she nodded toward Cinema Village, a repertory movie theater.

"This is a place we used to meet," said Lydia. "When one of us got in trouble at school, and they would try to keep us apart, we would come here and find each other in the back row. We'd hang out and neck like we were on a date."

She walked up to the box office, took a snapshot out of her purse, and showed it to the woman behind the glass partition.

"Have you seen this girl?"

The woman squinted at it then said, "Sure, she was the first person in today, twenty minutes before the program began. She's been here before. I've seen you, too."

"Is she still here?" Lydia asked.

The woman shrugged. "I just got back from my break, but talk to him, he's the one who sees all the action."

She indicated the kid who took the tickets, and Lydia showed him the same snapshot.

"Have you seen this girl?"

The kid looked and blinked and nodded his head.

"Yeah, she was here. She must have been here for a couple of hours, maybe longer. She stayed through the feature, and through intermission, and must have been well into the trailers for the second show when some guy in a big hurry came in and took her away."

"What did he look like?" asked Lydia, excited and nervous.

"Early forties. At first, I thought he was her dad, but he didn't look like a dad. Red hair, squinty eyes. She didn't seem happy to see him, and he was dragging her by the arm."

"Shit!" said Lydia. "That's Ricky! That means they've got her!"

"But that wasn't quite the end of it," said the kid. "When she got out into the street, she started screaming blue bloody murder. The guy was trying to manhandle her into a car that was double-parked— a red one—but there were some hardhats out there and they stepped in and broke it up. The guy cursed at them but the girl kept yelling and said that he'd tried to assault her. One of the hardhats waved to a police car that was coming crosstown, and the guy hightailed out of here in his vehicle. The first cop car took off after him, then another one came and the cops in that one spoke to the girl and took her away. She didn't want to go, but they were pretty insistent."

● ○ ●

Out on the street, Lydia was both relieved and angry.

"She's finally getting some street smarts," she said. "Okay, Mr. Detective, where would the cops take her?"

"From here, they'd take her to the 6th Precinct."

"And how do we find out what's happened to her?"

"By going there."

"Give me a break. How can I go there?"

"You can't. You're going to have to trust me."

"Are you joking? You're sticking with me. You're my insurance policy."

I remembered her mother talking about how winning the beauty contest had been her insurance policy. Had Marion Kravitz once looked like Lydia? It was hard to believe. But then it was hard to believe that Lydia, who had the face of a Piero della Francesca angel, could be mixed up in bomb making and God knows what else, and could have the sheer cojones to behave the way she was behaving right then.

But it was time for me to take over.

"If you really want to help Andrea," I said, "this is your only chance. They know me at the 6th Precinct, they'll talk to me. If Andrea's there, I can probably get to see her. If she was still carrying the gun, she'll have a lot of questions to answer. I don't know what I'll be able to do with any of that, but you'll have to let me try it. You have no other choice. I'm not going to promise you I'll never tell the cops what I know about you, but you have my word I won't squeal on you for the next couple of hours, and I'll stretch that out as long as I can."

As I spoke, Lydia reminded me, by tapping the side of her bag, that she had the gun trained on me.

"I don't trust you," she said.

I decided to test her, and reached for my cigarettes.

"Do I look like a dummy?" she asked. "I know you have a gun in there. Lucky you reached for the other pocket. And give me one of those while you're at it."

I did the time-honored Paul Henreid routine, and passed a lit Gauloise to Lydia.

"So how do I know I can trust you to take care of Andrea?" she asked.

"The other night," I said, "Andrea tried to seduce me. She did it for you. I didn't touch her, which wasn't easy."

Lydia actually smiled.

"I wouldn't do anything to hurt Andrea," I said. "I'm suggesting you let me walk away from here and go straight to the 6th Precinct to see what I can find out, and I'm also suggesting that you get as far away from here as you can. Though that may not be easy because by now I'm sure they've got people watching every train station and bus station in the city."

"Okay," she said. "I guess I have to trust you. But if you screw me, I swear I'll get you, from beyond the grave if necessary. But I'm not running away, because there's nowhere to go. In return for trusting me, you are going to get news to me, to let me know that Andrea is okay. That's the deal. Do you know that abandoned pier near the end of Bethune Street? Okay. I'll be there and I'll be expecting to hear from you. If you find her, bring her with you."

There was no way I was going to do that, but I wasn't about to argue about it either.

"I'll need that photo of Andrea," I said.

Lydia hesitated, took the snapshot from her purse, kissed it, and gave it to me.

● ● ●

At the 6th Precinct, Sergeant Morello was on desk duty. I showed him the picture.

"What's she to you, Novalis?" he asked.

"A straightforward missing persons case," I said.

"And she's the missing person?"

"No, she's a friend of the missing girl but I've reason to think she may know something about the latter's whereabouts."

(There's something about dealing with cops that makes me say things like "the latter's whereabouts.")

"I was showing this picture around," I went on, "at a few hangouts that both of them have been known to frequent. At Cinema Village they told me I might find her here. Seems there was a little bit of an incident there earlier today."

"So that's how you do things in the private sector," said Morello. "You spend your time going door to door flashing pictures of people who are not missing. Seems fucking perverted to me."

"Is she here?" I asked.

"She was here," he said, reluctantly. "A couple of the boys brought her in because there'd been a bit of a fracas and she'd accused some guy of grabbing her tits, but he had done a disappearing act and she refused to press charges…"

"So she's no longer here?"

"Do we have to do your work for you, Novalis?"

A police radio had been crackling in the background, and now, as I was about to leave, I caught an incoming 10-88. The caller reported that a red Pontiac, the subject of a vehicular pursuit, had crashed into a cart selling pretzels near Bowling Green. The driver had made a getaway on foot, but the trunk of the Pontiac had burst open in the crash and was found to contain small-caliber ordinance and devices that appeared to be attached to timing mechanisms. The bomb squad had been alerted.

That gave me a sick feeling in my stomach. Andrea could have been in that car, and it could have gone sky high.

I left the station house and walked toward Hudson Street. I had just reached the corner when somebody tugged on my jacket from behind.

Andrea.

She looked exhausted and beaten. I think she thought I was going to yell at her, but when she saw that I wasn't, she put her arms around my waist, rested her face against my shoulder and shed tears on my lapel.

"We've got to do some serious talking," I told her.

● ● ●

We went to a Korean grocery that had a couple of tables in the back. Andrea ate a Hershey bar and drank a Tab. I smoked another cigarette. I took out the snapshot Lydia had given me and showed it to her.

"You know where I got this from?" I said.

Her face lit up.

"Is she okay?"

"Physically, she's fine—but she's in a lot of trouble, from both sides of the law."

I told her about my recent adventures with Lydia, but left out where she was currently hiding.

"I've got to go to her," said Andrea. "How do we find her?"

"Right now," I told her, "we don't know where she is, and we're not going to look for her. You've just stepped out of the station house, and the cops always sense when something's out of whack. I spoke to the desk sergeant. I showed him that snapshot and told him I was looking for you. He wanted to know why so I had to shoot him a bit of a line. He told me you'd been released, but he was obviously more than a little curious."

"How did you know I was there?" Andrea asked.

"I traced you to Cinema Village and the kid who takes tickets told me what had happened. The point is, the cops didn't have any reason to hold you, but that doesn't mean they forgot about you the moment you stepped outside the station house. While I was talking to the cops, an alert came in. Jerry Pedrosian's car, presumably driven by the guy who tried to grab you, crashed with the police in pursuit. They found weapons and stuff in the trunk. That means that when they trace him and the car back to the report you just filed, you will be designated a person of interest. If you try to find Lydia, you are likely to lead the cops straight to her."

That registered.

"So what can I do?" she asked.

"We're going to find somewhere for you to stay out of sight, and you're going to stay there this time. But first there are things I need to know. How did Rick—that's the red-haired creep's name—know to find you at Cinema Village?"

"I wondered about that, but I think maybe I've figured it out. Do you remember I told you I once went to the movies with Lydia and Jerry? That was at Cinema Village. *Pierrot le Fou*. I remember that because they were crazy about that film. They said it was about life the way it should be lived—fast and dangerous. They'd seen it together four times that week, and Jerry said that that Jean-Luc Godard was the only film director worth shit. They especially loved the ending, when Belmondo blows himself up. Anyway, Jerry was ignoring me as usual, and Lydia was doing her best to include me in the conversation. She told Jerry that Cinema Village was our special place, where we went to hide out. He didn't seem interested, but I guess he filed the information away for future use."

That sounded plausible.

"Yeah, probably he sent Rick there to look for Lydia, and he found you instead. But how would Rick know you?"

"The afternoon Jerry Pedrosian intercepted me outside my apartment—before I came to your house—he had a bodyguard with him. Remember? I told you how this dude was patrolling the sidewalk out near the Women's House of Detention, like he was on the lookout for trouble. That was the guy who grabbed me this afternoon. I had your pistol in my bag. I was trying to get it out, but he was dragging me along and I couldn't. When we got to the street, he saw I was reaching for something and snatched the bag away from me. I kicked him and started screaming. That's when the hardhats came to my rescue, but the guy got away with your pistol. Sorry."

"Just as well. If the cops had found it on you, you would have been in big trouble."

She nodded.

"Okay," I said, "now what is it that you are supposed to know that Lydia says places you in danger? You must have some idea what that could be."

Andrea shook her head and looked thoroughly miserable.

"Think," I said. "Are there any secrets between you and Lydia that might have some bearing on the situation? Even things that don't necessarily seem to relate…"

She was becoming more miserable by the moment.

"Did she ever tell you anything about her relationship with Pedrosian? I mean, I don't care what they liked to do in bed— anything that was out of the usual?"

Andrea was crying now. It was time for me to bully her a little.

"I have to know—otherwise Christ knows what you're condemning Lydia to."

She wiped away a tear.

"Pedrosian had an affair with Lydia's mother," she said. "I promised I'd never tell a soul."

"Wonderful!" I said. "And when was this? Recently?"

Andrea shook her head.

"I don't know. A long time ago, I think. Lydia found out about it by accident—just before she came down here last weekend. She's not the only Teddington girl Pedrosian slept with. There's this girl Carla Reese who Lydia can't stand. A junior. She was Pedrosian's favorite a couple of years ago and he still finds time to fit her in once in a while. He boasted to her that he'd slept with Lydia *and* Lydia's mother, and then catty Carla blurted it out in the front of a bunch of girls in the school laundromat. When Lydia came down last week, she had a big row with her mother about it. That was right before she came to my apartment."

"Does her father know about this affair?"

"I don't know. I don't think so. There's a lot of secrets between those two."

"I don't get it," I said. "Lydia finds out about Pedrosian and her mother, but even so she's still planning to go ahead and meet him at the party, and she still gets jealous when he dances with some other girl?"

"You've got a lot to learn," said Andrea. "She told me she was planning to confront him, but when she saw him dancing with this other girl, that changed everything. All the resolve drained out of her. 'Water under the bridge,' she said. It's like he has some hold over her. Anyhow, she was in pretty deep with Pedrosian in all kinds of ways. She couldn't just walk away."

"But she did."

"Eventually, I guess."

"And anyway," I said, "even assuming that Pedrosian knew that you knew about the affair with Lydia's mom that hardly seems enough reason for you to be targeted."

I told her to sit tight while I made a call. The call was to my ex. I informed her that she was about to become a big sister for a few hours. Janice told me to go fuck myself. This was a matter of life and death, I said. That brought the same response, but I told her I'd be at her apartment in ten minutes.

As I finished my call, the *Post* delivery van was dropping off a special edition. There was a photo of Jerry Pedrosian— "self-styled artist"—covering the entire front page along with a banner headline: WANTED! I took the paper back to show Andrea. The story inside said that the remains of at least one victim, believed to be female, had been found at the scene. Apparently, either Lucy or Crystal had attained the ultimate high. It was believed that two other women and as many as four men were at large, though one of the men was thought to be holding hostages in a bank on Lower Broadway, after crashing his car during the course of a police pursuit. The only person named in the story was Pedrosian, which got Andrea excited till I told her that I knew for a fact that the police had Lydia's name. After all, I'd given it to them.

Then I told Andrea that I was taking her to my ex's house. She seemed shocked.

"It's only three blocks away from here," I explained.

"But your ex-wife?"

"Not ideal, but she's the best we can do. Don't be put off by her manner. She has a problem relating to cute girls who remind her of what she looked like ten years ago. The important thing is she can be trusted. If she has the radio on, or the TV, which is very likely, and there's news about the explosion, or any of this stuff, act dumb. You didn't hear a thing about it till that very moment."

She nodded, and we set off for Janice's place, which had once been mine, just around the corner from the Blue Mill Tavern. As we turned onto Lampwick Street, a car pulled up alongside us. It was an unmarked police car and in the front passenger seat was Detective Campbell.

"Who's the attractive young lady?" he asked, through the open window.

"This is Andrea, my niece from Poughkeepsie," I said.

"She must take after the other side of the family," he said. "Much too pretty to have any of your genes."

Andrea made nice.

"Are you going back to your office?" asked Campbell.

"Not today," I said. "I'm showing Andrea the town."

"Tell him not to leave out the zoo," said Campbell, "and take a look at police headquarters if you get a chance. A masterpiece in the manner of the French baroque."

He gave Andrea an avuncular leer then turned his attention back to me.

"So you're not going to your office?" he said, as if this hadn't already been established. "That's too bad. You could have done me a favor."

And with that he was off. We continued to Janice's. She answered the door with a cigarette dangling from her lips—a signal to her temporary ward that she was a no-nonsense dame—simultaneously appraising Andrea like a 7th Avenue fur buyer checking over mink pelts that he suspected of being dyed coney.

"I'm sure you two will get along," I said.

"Yeah, maybe we can play Chutes and Ladders," said Janice. "How long will this be for?"

"Not long, I hope."

"Keep it brief," said Janice. "I might get a sudden urge to go to the library, or something."

"While you're there," I said, "find yourself a nice crime novel."

SEVENTEEN

The riverfront was Desolation Row. Through traffic—
headed south toward Brooklyn, or north toward the boonies—
rattled along a rapidly decaying section of elevated highway getting ready to collapse under its own weight. West Street was a
wasteland and most of the piers that jutted out into the Hudson
had been abandoned. Some had disappeared entirely, except for
a few rotting pilings, some had been cleared down to the deck,
while others supported ramshackle structures in varying degrees
of decay.

The pier where Lydia had said I would find her fell into the
last category. It had once been the Manhattan terminal of a ferry
line connecting the city with Hoboken. Now, the derelict shed
that once sheltered passengers from sun and rain had become
an after-dark theater of dreams for gay men, and long-distance
truck drivers with a taste for drag queens. By day, it was mostly
deserted except for rodents and seagulls. I made my entry by
squeezing through a jagged gap in a wall of rusting corrugated
steel. The interior was divided up by scattered partitions—those
that had not yet collapsed—and the irregular spaces were littered

with bits of fallen masonry, broken furniture, the dilapidated remains of a ticket kiosk, mattresses dragged there from the streets to facilitate furtive sexual encounters, a dead dog, empty pint bottles, discarded food cartons, and yellowing newspapers fluttering in the breeze that wafted through broken windows. Columns of sunlight poured through holes in the roof, and here and there the water that lapped against the piles on which the pier rested could be glimpsed through gaps in the wooden deck. The ultimate B-movie set.

I took the Ruger from my pocket and chambered a round. No sign of Lydia, but then I did not expect her to be out in full view doing yoga. I moved slowly and carefully onto the pier, pausing every few feet to check behind some obstruction or another. No sign of life. I could understand Lydia being cautious, but the stillness—punctuated by a constant drip, drip, drip that always seemed close by—was not easy on the nerves.

Then suddenly she was there. She stepped out from behind a pillar and planted herself in my path.

"For God's sake put that gun away," she said. "I thought we'd decided to trust each other."

"I'll hang on to it for the moment," I said.

"Do what you want. The important thing is did you find Andrea?"

"Matter of fact, she found me."

"And is she okay?"

"She's shaken, but she's fine."

"Where is she?"

"I don't know."

Lydia's face froze into a mask of anger.

"You're lying! Where is she?" she said, a snarl in her voice.

"I can't tell you," I said, "because that's dangerous information."

I felt something hard against the back of my neck. The muzzle of a gun. I would have been willing to bet it was a Ruger.

"There's been a lot of dangerous information flying around," said a voice that was all too familiar.

Jerry Pedrosian. He told me to drop my gun and patted me down.

"When I told Gabe Kravitz to hire a detective to locate Lydia," he continued, "it didn't occur to me at first to suggest you. Then I remembered that you'd been on my case once before. You hadn't been able to figure out what I was involved with that time. Why would you do any better this time? You'd make the perfect fall guy."

That hurt, but I couldn't let it show.

"You mean the Pol Smit case?" I said. "Those collages you faked for him were halfway decent."

The muzzle of the gun poked into my neck. I sensed that I had managed to touch a nerve.

"So if you knew about them, why didn't you have me busted?"

"Sometimes you have to let the small fry go."

Again, the back of my neck received a massage. Meanwhile, Lydia stepped forward to scoop up the weapon I'd dropped. Strangely, I felt completely calm. I guess genetic memory kicked in and reminded me that if you find yourself in a cave with a pair of saber-toothed tigers your only hope is to pretend that you're not scared shitless. And anyway, if the end came, it would all be over pretty quickly.

Something a little closer to logic told me not to satisfy the expectations of my captors. I was dying to know what Pedrosian meant by saying that he had told Gabriel Kravitz to hire me to look for his daughter, and I was sure he was dying to tell me, but I was damned if I was going to give him the satisfaction of asking. Instead, I tried a different tack.

"I guess by now," I said, "that you regret having got me involved."

"How so?" he said.

"If it hadn't been for me," I continued, "You wouldn't have had to leave your first safe house. I imagine it must have been a pain in the ass, and a bit dicey, moving those explosives from one place to the other at short notice. And then look what happened."

"You're overestimating your importance in the scheme of things," said Pedrosian. "That's what happens with tiny minds."

I just kept going.

"Remind me to tell you sometime about the phone call that tipped me off to that location. A woman's voice…"

Did I imagine it, or did Lydia's eyes narrow a millimeter?

"The move had been planned long before you stumbled upon the building," said Pedrosian, sounding a shade defensive.

"Really? I would have thought that that was a bad time to have to make that kind of move—just as you were about to carry out your first bombing."

"You don't know shit," said Pedrosian.

"I know that someone got blown to bits this morning."

"Crystal was careless," said Pedrosian. "It was the stupid bitch's own fault."

"How many times had you fucked that kid?" I asked.

I continued to watch Lydia's face as I said this. It didn't betray much. Her nostrils flared slightly, and she was breathing a little heavily, but the pistol was steady in her hand.

"Let me show you something," said Pedrosian. "Walk over that way, toward that window. The one through which—God, I love the fucking irony!—you can see the Statue of Liberty."

I did as he told me, his gun now in the small of my back. Behind a fallen beam, I saw two bodies lying facedown—Homer, the hippie kid, and one of his so-called sisters. Each had been shot once in the back of the head. Now Pedrosian stepped out from behind me so that I could see him for the first time. He was wearing shorts and a Hawaiian shirt, which seemed weirdly incongruous, and there was a crazy grin on his face. I'd seen kissing cousins of that grin before, usually when he was about to spill beer on someone to start a bar fight. This one was a lot scarier.

"You see," he said, "if Crystal had survived the explosion I'd have had to deal with her the same way. These kids had outlived their usefulness. They were out to save themselves."

"An act of treason…"

"They were creatures of limited intelligence," said Pedrosian, "unlike the lovely Lydia."

"And how come she wasn't in the house when it blew?" I asked.

"I asked myself the same thing," said Pedrosian. "Seems she had said something about going out for a little air. She often does things like that. Sometimes she's gone for hours."

Lydia's response was a slight smile.

"Yeah, sometimes she just stands around outside my window," I said.

"Oh, that part was just teasing," said Pedrosian. "Do you remember we once got into a bit of a face-off at the Cedar Tavern, you and I?"

I recalled that there had been something of a confrontation at the Cedar, back in the days when you could still find the abstract expressionists and the beats getting smashed out of their skulls there. I don't remember what it was about, but I was with a girl that night and wasn't about to take Pedrosian's bait.

"As I remember it," he said, "you backed off, and ever since, I've had you figured as someone who could be easily unsettled, if you know what I mean? I thought that since we'd gotten you involved in this little game of ours—this very serious little game—that we might have some fun with you. All work and no play makes Jerry a dull boy. I hope you found it fun, too."

"But are you sure Lydia was always playing by your rules?" I said.

That caused a flicker of concern, but the grin came back in an instant.

"We're the kind of people who make up the rules as we go along," said Pedrosian. "Isn't that right, sweetheart?"

Lydia just smiled.

"Lydia and I have a very special, very tight relationship," said Pedrosian.

"Rooted in the fact that you fucked her mother," I said, making it sound as brutish as I could. "Which one was better?"

Lydia did not flinch.

"You are so unbelievably fucking bourgeois," said Pedrosian, the grin morphing for a moment into a sneer.

"How come," I asked, "a guy like you didn't just tell Lydia about that little episode? I hear that she had to find out from a girl at school."

Now there was a flash of anger in Lydia's eyes.

"I like to play games," said Pedrosian. "It was sweet to be able to think, 'I did this to your mother, too, babe, and you don't even know about it.' But you're right, Novalis. I let it play out too long. Lydia got on my case over that, but we've had all that out. She's cool with it now, aren't you, sweetheart?"

Her response was the look of someone who has just bitten into a sour grape.

"It was a long time ago," said Pedrosian. "The Kravitzes had just moved to the city, and Marion had found out that hubby had some very kinky habits. She had thought they were just the games he liked to play with her—creepy dressing-up games—but then she found out there was much more to it than that. She was looking for something to lift her spirits. She started to hang out on the art scene. I was the new young star in the firmament. Voila!"

"Knock it off," said Lydia, but Pedrosian paid no attention.

"Imagine my surprise," he continued, "when I paid my annual visit to that noble institution of higher learning, Teddington College, and discovered this delicious creature seated in lotus position on the floor of the auditorium. She seemed so innocent, as you must have noticed, but when I talked to some of my informants there, I found that, to the contrary, she was anything but. Boys, they told me, girls, too—at least one member of the faculty of each sex—and she'd only been there a couple of months. I was enchanted by her intuitive understanding of my agenda, though her tolerance for dialectic was low, and I would have to describe her as more of an instinctive anarchist. The Dadaists would have loved her. I could imagine her at the Café Voltaire in 1916, performing some obscene cabaret song for the amusement of Tristan Tzara, and the rest of that crowd."

"For God's sake, shut up," said Lydia. "You're not teaching a course now."

"But that's exactly what I am doing," said Pedroslan. "I'm providing our friend here with an education. I admit we may have failed in our ultimate goals, this time, but our example will live on. We are part of history now, babe. We will be remembered for pointing the way to a stateless society. They'll talk about us the way they talk now about John Reed and Emma Goldman.

Mr. Novalis should be given the opportunity to understand what the future holds. Alive or dead, he can spread the word—let our complacent fellow Americans know they are not immune to the winds of change—and those winds will not be gentle. Let them understand that change will be brought about ruthlessly and violently, with terror striking from the skies and reaching into the cities and towns and every last Appalachian hamlet."

He was beginning to sound like Gary Cooper in some twisted inversion of a Frank Capra movie.

"For God's sake," said Lydia, "let's just show him and be done with it."

She turned and began to walk away from me, having indicated that I should follow. Pedrosian fell in behind me, the muzzle of the gun in the small of my back once again. I began to wonder who was in charge around here. We walked maybe fifty feet farther out onto the pier, to a spot where an old pine door lay flat on the deck. Lydia stopped there and gestured, with the pistol she was holding, that I should move the door. It wasn't heavy and I was able to push it aside with my foot. Underneath was a large hole in the decking. Floating faceup in the putrid water below, one ankle tied to a piling, was the body of a man. Lydia's father, my client, Gabriel Kravitz.

"Shocked?" asked Lydia. "He stole my childhood. The bastard made me pregnant when I was still a kid. He was my father, so I thought I was supposed to forgive him, but I warned him never to lay a finger on Andrea. If he had listened to me, he might still be alive."

The words were chilling, but not half as chilling as the composure—serenity even—with which they were spoken. I remembered now how I had been struck by Kravitz's reference to Andrea's "nice little place in the Village."

"When was he killed?" I asked.

It didn't look as if he'd been in the water long, and I saw now that there was a jagged wound to his neck. I wondered who had killed him. For all her composure, I couldn't picture Lydia slitting her own father's throat.

"Perhaps you're getting the wrong picture," said Lydia. "He was in the house this morning when it blew. His throat was ripped open by flying glass."

"It wouldn't have been cool," said Pedrosian, "if his body was found and identified—that would have given too much away. So, with help from Rick and Lanny, and taking advantage of the confusion—there was smoke and dust everywhere—I managed to get him into the truck we had parked outside. The explosions had cracked its windshield, but it was still drivable so Rick and Lanny brought the body here. This had been designated as a rendezvous if anything went wrong."

"But what was he doing in the house?" I asked.

"He was delivering some Czechoslovakian plastic explosives I'd ordered him to get a hold of for me."

"You mean he was in on the whole thing?"

"One of the flaws of capitalism," said Pedrosian, "is that plutocrats who attain the level of oppression achieved by Gabe Kravitz are very vulnerable to blackmail. When I found out about his taste for jailbait, I knew I had the son of a bitch. It was wonderful to see the arrogance drain out of him when I confronted him. And it's not just been Lydia and her beloved Andrea. There's a fourteen-year-old on Staten Island whose mother has been receiving handsome payoffs. I could go on, but the point is that I needed explosives, he had access to them, and I was in a position to send him to the joint for a couple of lifetimes. As a dialectical materialist, I don't believe in luck or an afterlife. But, shit, somebody's been looking after me—Trotsky, or Bakunin, or one of those beautiful muthafuckas."

"And why did you have Kravitz hire me to find Lydia?"

"Because, whatever happened, it would provide him with a cover story when the shit hit the fan. Why would the guy pay someone to look for her if he fucking knew where she was? It was a beautiful idea. Not that I cared a shit about him, but if he's okay, I'm okay."

"So, I'm hired," I said. "Why bother to have someone try to push me under a train? Kind of counterproductive."

"I just wanted to scare the shit out of you."

"All part of the game?"

"All part of the game. You'll remember there was also someone on the spot to grab you before you fell. I think of everything."

"And when someone shot at me in the Bronx, outside your aunt Ida's apartment?"

Pedrosian laughed. A crazy man's laugh.

"Someone shot at you in the Bronx? So what's new about that? It wasn't anyone from my combat cell. And how is Aunt Ida, by the way?"

"She hates your guts. And what about the call to the police about the man with a gun in my office?"

"That was one time that Lydia's little friend Andrea was useful. She was calling the message service to let Lydia know where she was. In one call, she told Lydia that she'd found something in her bag and had passed it on to you—she hoped that was okay. She didn't say what it was, but it wasn't hard to guess."

I was learning a lot, but it was getting me nowhere. I had to find some way of stirring things up.

"I suppose you realize," I said, "that Lydia wanted me to find her?"

I was hoping that there was at least a scrap of truth in that statement. Pedrosian's response was not what I expected.

"Do you think I don't know that? She's been a very bad girl. She's so hung up on that stupid little tart of hers—doesn't want her to get hurt. I've been getting quite concerned about the lovely Lydia. She's talented, but she lets her mind wander from the task at hand. That's one reason I sent her to haunt you. I wanted to see how she would react to the temptation—and you, too, of course. I was pretty sure the two of you were together earlier today, and she confessed as much—but it doesn't matter. She came back to Jerry. That's what counts."

While he spoke, Lydia didn't so much as blink.

It was at this point that it struck me how, from Pedrosian's point of view, this *had* all been a game—a dangerous one that had spun wildly out of control. He had been on a fantasy power trip for years, going to places like Teddington and seducing credulous girls with fairy tales about artistic uprisings and cultural revolution. It was how he got his rocks off, but there wasn't much more to it than that. Pedrosian was no dedicated revolutionary. But then he had run up against Lydia, and the ante was upped. Lydia was not just the docile acolyte that I had at first assumed her to be. She was a tough cookie who, despite appearances, had had plenty of opportunity to work up a powerful head of anger, especially against her parents. This anger had played spectacularly into Pedrosian's fantasies, especially when he found that Gabriel Kravitz was choice blackmail material and had access to the explosives that he so cherished for the harebrained conceit that was beginning to take shape in his head. Blow something up—the ultimate happening. That was what Pedrosian had had in mind, a stupendous performance piece, something that took place in the gap between art and life, as Bob Rauschenberg famously put it. The problem was that, as the plan took shape, real life had edged out art entirely. My guess was that, under the crazy exterior, Pedrosian was petrified. Maybe he had been hoping I'd find him before everything blew up in his face.

That time had passed, and now mine was fast running out.

A telephone rang, and I saw that, a few feet away, was the briefcase radiophone that I had seen before on Ladies Lane. Pedrosian walked over and picked it up.

"Yes, Lanny...You did? Good work. That's too bad..."

I'd forgotten about Lanny.

"Lanny says the pigs got Rick," said Pedrosian, matter-of-factly, still holding the receiver. "There was a shoot-out in a bank. He died in a temple of capitalism, but he took at least one pig with him."

He spoke into the phone again.

"What was that address? 133 Lampwick Street. Thanks for that, Lanny. No, no, leave her where she is. I'll take care of this personally. See you in Vladivostok, comrade..."

How the hell had Lanny found that out? 133 Lampwick Street was Janice's address.

"I see," said Pedrosian, approaching me, his pistol waggling ominously, "that you're familiar with that address. But then, of course, you used to live there. I've been there myself, a few times, but I could never remember the street number. Didn't matter, though, because it has that bright blue front door. All I had to do was go to the bright blue door and ring the bell. You weren't at home at the time, of course."

He turned to Lydia.

"Did I ever tell you, sweetheart, I used to fuck Novalis's old lady? She was a good fuck, too, as Alex here will attest, but he and Janice weren't seeing eye to eye at the time. You know how these things creep into a marriage—or maybe you don't—those little yens for pastures *nouvelles*."

He turned back to me.

"That's another reason I recommended you for the job, Novalis. After fucking your wife, I felt I owed you a favor. This morning, when things started to go wrong, it occurred to me that there was a good chance that our paths would cross, and I might need an insurance policy. What or who better than Janice, I thought. Great ass, by the way. So I had Lanny check her out, just in case I needed to—how shall I put it?—get a hold of her. Of course, I'd forgotten the house number, but luckily the door is still the same color. By the way, is that color approved by the community board? Well, Lanny just got around to checking. He rang the doorbell and found Janice was in. He said there was someone else there, too. Lydia's little friend Andrea is hiding out there. Isn't that convenient? I think it's almost time to pay her a visit."

Lydia looked at me.

"Is that true?"

"He's just bluffing," I said.

She looked back at Pedrosian, not sure who to believe. Pedrosian laughed and cracked me across the side of the head with the pistol. Lydia winced.

"What I don't get," I said to her, "is why you came back to this creep when you know that yesterday he tried to run Andrea down in the street. You told me you couldn't forgive him for that. And then his goon tried to drag her out of the movie theater How could you let him get away with that?"

Pedrosian hit me again, this time in the stomach, with his fist.

Lydia pointed her gun at my head.

"I had to come back to Jerry," said Lydia, quietly, menacingly.

Pedrosian laughed.

"I just had to," Lydia continued.

"There. I told you," sneered Pedrosian. "She can't stay away from me."

"I had to come back," said Lydia, "…to take care of business…"

Without any show of emotion, she swung the gun away from me, toward Pedrosian, and pulled the trigger. The first slug caught Pedrosian smack in the groin. His eyes popped wide open, and he folded forward. She fired again, hitting him full in the face. He spat out blood and splinters of teeth, then collapsed onto the floor. Lydia swung the gun back toward me.

"Get the keys out of his pocket then dump him into the river with my father."

"I don't know if he's dead," I said.

She fired two more shots into Pedrosian's head. Gulls squawked and scattered.

"Satisfied?" she asked.

I fished the keys from Pedrosian's pocket.

Lydia stood over the body, staring down at the remains of the bloody face, then turned away and threw up.

"Just leave him there," she said. "Let's go find Andrea."

EIGHTEEN

Lydia directed me to a black Dodge pickup truck with
a cracked windshield, parked under the elevated highway. She
didn't bother to hide the little Ruger that was still trained on me,
but no one was around to see it anyway.

"You drive," she said.

We got in, and before I turned the key in the ignition I asked,
"Are you sure you want to do this?"

She smiled—the first real smile I had seen from her. It was
the kind that can get a girl's name onto a movie contract.

"Do I really have to answer that question?" she said.

"So what's under the tarp in the back of the truck?" I asked.

"Oh, that?" she said. "Try to avoid potholes."

I started the motor.

"Do you want to know why I killed him?" she asked. "Well,
there's more than one reason. As soon as I knew that Jerry knew
where Andrea was, I had to do it. I couldn't bear the thought of
him touching her, or even looking at her. He was always jealous
of Andrea because he knew how tight we were. He thought of
her as his rival. He would have taken his revenge on her in some

horrible way, so I had to shoot him. But I would have killed him anyway. I've already had one man steal my childhood, and now this one stole my future. I guess in some ways it was my fault."

"That's what they wanted you to believe," I told her.

I pulled out onto West Street and began to work my way crosstown.

"Why did you stick with Pedrosian so long?" I asked.

"For a while, I didn't think anything was going to happen. We were talking about revolution, but it was fantasy. Jerry was having too much of a good time to risk everything by doing something that could blow up in his face. More fun to talk about it in the interludes between fucking. Then one night I made a big mistake. We'd dropped some acid, and as I was coming down from the trip I got weepy and told him what my father had done to me. At first he thought I was still tripping out, but then he realized what I had told him was for real. He already knew about my father's demolition company and he'd fantasized about me somehow getting a hold of explosives. No way. But knowing what he now knew—and without telling me—he confronted my father and told him he would go to the papers with the story. My father said he would deny everything, but he was scared enough to agree to a meeting in Jerry's studio. The studio has a sleeping loft and Jerry hid me up there, telling me that I should stay out of sight and I was going to witness something mind-blowing. I presumed it was one of Jerry's games. When my father walked through the door, I thought I would die. Jerry laid it on the line for him, and he called his bluff, too. He had guessed that I probably wasn't the only one. My father broke down. I can't tell you what it was like for me to see this man—who had been the authority figure in my life, and who had abused me for years—groveling. I guess that's why I hung in with Jerry as long as I did."

"And what about your father and Andrea?"

She turned away from me and stared out the side window for a while, then she took a deep breath.

"I had only one secret from Andrea," she said, "and you know what it was. She always had a sexy little bod. I would see my father sniffing around her, and knowing what he'd done to me, I was terrified. I told him point blank, once—if you ever touch Andrea I'll kill you. He thought that was pretty funny at the time. Well, the bottom line is that he stayed away from her until I left town to go to college. Until then, Andrea and I were always together when he saw her. Soon after I'd started at Teddington—about the time Jerry was teaching his course there—my father shows up at Andrea's apartment. He tells her he's brought her a gift, expensive lingerie he'd hauled back from Hong Kong or somewhere tacky like that. She doesn't know how to react. He says, 'Aren't you going to try it on for me?' She says she doesn't think that would be appropriate. He gets himself wound up, reminds her of all the presents he's given her over the years, all the expensive trips he's taken her along on. She starts to feel bad. She says, okay, she'll try on the lingerie, but then he has to leave. After all, she thinks, he's seen me in a bikini—what's the big deal? Andrea's a bit naive that way. She goes into the bedroom to change. He waits till she comes out. Do I need to go on? She said she felt sorry for him. Can you imagine? And, of course, she was scared to tell me. Finally, she did, though—last weekend, at her apartment, just before I was due to meet Jerry. We were sitting on the bed where it had happened.

"By that time, Jerry had got my father wrapped up in his crazy scheme. He'd already delivered enough explosives to blow up City Hall. Andrea looks at me with those big eyes of hers. For some reason I couldn't bring myself to tell her that she's not the only one, but I assure her it's not her fault, and I promise her I'll take care of things—whatever I meant by that."

She reached into her bag and took out a letter. It was addressed to Andrea.

"Give this to her, will you? It explains a lot of stuff she should know."

"If we're going to see her, why don't you give it to her yourself? Or just tell her?"

"Too much to tell all at once. I'd rather she reads it when I'm not there."

● ● ●

We were almost at Janice's apartment. For the first time I could remember, there was a parking place almost directly in front of the building. Lydia fixed her hair in the mirror behind the sun visor, then we walked up the stoop to the blue door, the little Ruger still clutched in Lydia's fist. I rang the bell and Janice answered it.

"Well, at least you didn't take too long," she said.

Then she saw the bloody gash on my cheek, and the gun in Lydia's hand, and tried to slam the door. I blocked it with my foot and forced it open with my shoulder.

"We're just coming in for a few minutes," said Lydia, "then I'll go."

She pushed past Janice who just gaped at my face.

"She didn't do it," I told her.

Andrea must have heard Lydia's voice. When she saw it really was her, she screamed for joy. Lydia ran to her and they embraced. Then Lydia waved the gun at Janice and me and said, "Give us five minutes alone. Don't worry. I'm not going to take her anywhere. She's been through enough already."

Janice gave me her best helpless look, and I led her back into the back parlor and closed the door.

"What's going on?" she hissed.

"If this plays out as it supposed to," I said, "these girls are going to have a little reunion and then the blonde's going to turn herself in to the cops."

"She's got a gun!"

"I noticed. Just try to stay quiet for a few minutes."

The door between us and the living room was a solid piece of craftsmanship that had been there for a hundred years or more. You couldn't hear much through it, except some nervous laughter, some sobbing, the occasional cliché—"I'll be okay...Don't worry about me...This is for the best."

Lydia was doing most of the talking. After maybe ten minutes, I heard her call out, in a louder voice, "Whatever you do, do not follow me. Promise?"

Then I heard the front door close, and I heard Andrea call out, "No..."

I stepped into the living room and saw her standing at the window.

"Is she turning herself in?" I asked.

"I don't know," said Andrea. "She said she was going to *Pierrot le Fou.*"

I knew what that meant.

I flew across the room and pulled Andrea to the ground just a moment before the truck exploded into a ball of fire.

NINETEEN

For the second time in my life, I spent the night in a cell, and for several days after that, I fielded a barrage of questions from NYPD detectives, the FBI, and other interested parties. Emerging from one of these grillings, I ran into Detective Campbell. He said he'd been meaning to look me up anyway.

"Too bad about your friend Olga," he said.

"What happened to Olga?" I asked.

"I wish I could have let her go," he said, "but it's my job to protect the citizens of this great metropolis from moral turpitude and flagrant perversity, though, to tell the truth, I don't know who I was protecting from moral turpitude unless it was the johns who were paying her fifty an hour to have her tie them up and tickle them with a bullwhip. But, hey, this is New Amsterdam not Amsterdam, and prostitution is illegal here, right? I had to bust her."

"So that's why I've seen so much of you lately?"

"Well, that's one reason. Olga asked me, by the way, to tell you that you'll have to wait for a while, but the offer still stands."

Andrea Marshall had a rough ride. Her parents put her into Greenholme—a so-called progressive facility in Connecticut. She signed herself out after a couple of years, went back to school somewhere in Virginia, graduated with a major in psychology, married some guy with a job in local television news, and had a kid. She came to see me once, to show me that she was all right. At twenty-something she was more beautiful than she had been when I first set eyes on her. She said she wanted to thank me, I never quite figured out for what. The marriage didn't pan out, but I heard that afterward she had a girlfriend, a veterinarian, who helped her bring up the kid.

I hope the memory of the exploding truck doesn't unreel in her mind too often, and that she can sometimes get through a night without hearing Lydia say, "Whatever you do, do not follow me…"

As Belmondo mutters, the moment before the dynamite detonates:

"Merde!"

About the Author

Photograph by Jonathan Mills, 2012

Christopher Finch was born and raised on the island of Guernsey in the British Channel Islands. He lived in London and Paris before moving to New York City in the late 1960s, the setting of *Good Girl, Bad Girl.* After working as a freelance writer and artist in New York for more than two decades, he moved to Los Angeles, where he continues to write and make art. Christopher has mounted one-man shows in both New York and Los Angeles, and his work has been included in museum exhibitions. He has occasionally written for television; his Judy Garland biography, *Rainbow*, was made into a movie for television. He is married to Linda Rosenkrantz, who is an author and the cofounder of the website nameberry.com. They have a daughter named Chloe.